Wyck'd You

for Roy
HRH 2014.

The Whitborough novels are one story spread across five books. It is the story of a long lost treasure, two curses and a community coming apart at the seams. There is death, there is diarrhoea and there are demons. For these reasons, the books should not be left in the vicinity of impressionable children – or people with nervous dispositions.

The author would like to state he does not condone cruelty to werewolves, banshees or Mini's.

Alistair Lavers is fifty five and is still annoying people. He rides an old motorcycle made from sparks and girders that sounds like an apocalypse in a scrapyard. He lives in a house full of draughts and spiders. His background is in the arts, the military and the occult. Occasionally, someone spits out their coffee whilst reading one of his books.

Wyck'd You

The Whitborough Novels

Alistair Lavers

Matador
9 Priory Business Park,
Wistow Road, Kibworth Beauchamp,
Leicestershire, LE8 0RX
Tel: 0116 279 2299
Email: books@troubador.co.uk
Web: www.troubador.co.uk/matador
Twitter: @matadorbooks

ISBN 978 1838592 196

British Library Cataloguing in Publication Data.
A catalogue record for this book is available from the British Library.

Printed and bound in the UK by TJ International, Padstow, Cornwall
Typeset in 11pt Aldine401 BT by Troubador Publishing Ltd, Leicester, UK

Matador is an imprint of Troubador Publishing Ltd

Dedicated to J.R.R Tolkein.
One of my Grandfather's friends in academia.

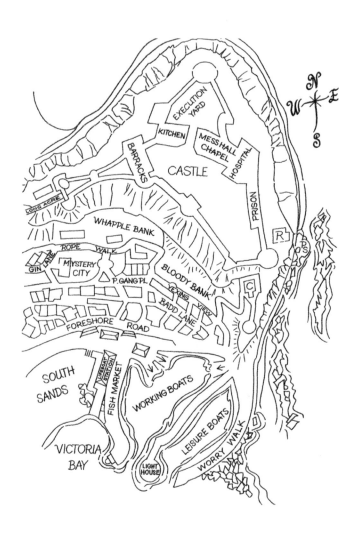

Contents

Photo Credits

Front Cover
Kelly 'Mysty' Keefe as 'Fenella Parrish' by www.
steverimages

Inside Front
@afamiliarnightmare as 'Michael Oak' by Hannah
Stewart MUA/
Photographer @gothicrosebeauty facebook.com/
gothicrosebeauty/

Inside Rear
The Vikings MCC, by themselves

Back Cover
Main picture, 'Mystic' Margo Jackson as 'Violet Penrose'
by Simon Ellery Photography
Penny and Stigg of the BADCOW commune

Art Direction and Graphic Design
Alistair Lavers. www.alistairlavers.co.uk

Prologue

Talk of the Town

If one were to conduct a simple survey and ask the question 'Are cities more interesting places than towns?', the vast majority of people would say cities, without a moment's hesitation. They could not be more wrong.

Whitborough-on-Sea is a typical English seaside town of around 130,000 souls in the county of Yorkshire. It exists on the edge, figuratively and literally, of civilisation and geography.

Whitborough survives on the many small commercial exchanges, voluntary (purchases) and involuntary (fines and taxes), which maintain the streets and shops of small-town England; on the ingenuity of its people (to avoid those second-category involuntary exchanges); and on tourism. It also has a self-serving agricultural sector and four good-sized garden centres.

Social scientists and clinical psychologists love garden centres. The reasonably conscientious careerists amongst them would never consider retiring to a town with fewer than three. Some unenlightened people might call this snobbery, but anyone who has come to the end of a career that put them in direct contact with unlucky, unwise or downright-hostile members of society could soon dispel that illusion.

There exists a little-known rating system, which is unknown to the public, and shared carefully only amongst the most cultured and worldly wise veterans of social services departments, health service providers, civil servants and local government. It is known as the 'bay-tree index' and it grades provincial towns (Pop.150,000 or fewer) by the number of garden centres they have. If there are four or more, this indicates a contented, settled community; three indicates a town moving towards respectability; two is typical in less-prosperous commuter towns with a higher proportion of rented properties; one garden centre means you are living in an area of social depravation; and a town with none is, by any reasonable definition, a war zone.

Over the course of one bank holiday weekend, Whitborough suddenly became the only war zone with four garden centres. It would have been no greater shock to the town than if its guests had been a Viking raiding party that had arrived on a sunny afternoon, burned down the lifeboat station, robbed the arcades and hacked down anyone who was unwise enough to object. What actually happened was worse than that, because, in front of a packed crowd on Victoria Bay, HMS *Heddon* and its helicopter had exploded after being hit by a cannonball from a Civil War siege cannon. Fortunately, the terrible events of the Easter weekend had begun to thin out the instigators of this most terrible episode. Peace and normality would soon return to the Yorkshire coast, but not before some very painful and bloody servings of cold justice.

Once Whitborough had returned to its normal state of grace, everyone that was respectable could once more contemplate visiting their local garden centre to purchase some French lavender, and have absolute faith that they were in no danger of being shot or engraved by shrapnel.

Unless, of course, they were on the moors, where the danger is a very different kind of animal (see Chapter One). But no one is going to warn any visitors about that –unless they want to stay in category two (*paragraph 3*) all their lives and go shopping in a flak jacket.

In Whitborough, the tourist is king, as long as his wallet is open. There are no great mines, shipyards or steelworks; no motorway or mainline railway connections; no grand museums or galleries; no great shopping avenues; and no rich municipal halls. It has no stadiums or theatre – except the one that was burned down by local gangster 'Mad' Mel Hazard to make way for a casino.

Whitborough once had a thriving fishing port and fish-processing plant, until Prime Minister Edward Heath signed away the exclusive rights to Britain's fishing grounds in exchange for membership of the Common Market. Heath had a yacht, Morning Cloud, but there is no evidence that he ever did any fishing. Had the captains of England's trawler fleet been allowed to exchange their vessels for U-boats, he would never have made it out of the twelve-mile limit again.

If anyone in Whitborough became wealthy, it was the result of hard work and sacrifice, or a good brain. Luck was not sought or expected, except by those poor individuals who are hopeless with money. But what becomes of those who have wealth thrust upon them, by accident or by revelation? What becomes of those whose sudden wealth is so unlucky and toxic that they begin to dream and, ultimately, fight to regain their old lives before disaster strikes?

This is the story of the Treasure of the Mar del Norte, accident-prone occultists, a record shop staff team like no other, a brash medium called Elsie, a procession of hopeless werewolves, a punk commune, the over confident forces of law and order, three resentful demons, and a very dirty dog.

First, a warning – in the tradition of Dennis Wheatley: on no account should the reader progress past this introduction– if it is after midnight– without the comfort of a water pistol of holy water and a small dish of rock salt. A steadying glass of malt (hello Ruth) or a comforting brandy would certainly help to take the edge off any strange noises or footsteps that may approach as these pages are turned. And if, suddenly, you should catch the scent of paella or chilli oil, find the sanctuary of a church as fast as you can. Good exorcists are busy people.

The discovery of Whitborough' s old treasure had not been lucky for its new guardians. It was not going to make an English count of Monte Cristo– or a new duke of Westminster. To date, it had only made a great many new ghosts. A mood of anxiety, foreboding and dread dogged the minds of the remaining members of the 'Fellowship of Gold', whose initial delight at finding themselves rich beyond their wildest dreams was long gone. The treasure needed to be reclaimed. There was just one problem for the man who had uncovered it: he was not at all sure how he was going to *put it back*.

Derek Beautimann – of Beautimann, Buerk and Trippe, and the grand wizard and master of ceremonies for the Black Hand Coven – was a hunted man. And he was running out of time…

Chapter One

Wuthering Frights

The longest stretch of road through the north-eastern uplands of the North Yorkshire Moors offers the brave and adventurous traveller a view of one of the wildest landscapes anywhere in Britain. From the cracked flagstone pavement of the old mail-coach stop at the Hole of Horcum to the towering rock walls of Weare Topping, there lies a panorama of such morbid magnetism and grand desolation that the rate of accidents for unaccompanied motor vehicles in good clear conditions is actually higher than when the road is at its busiest in peak season.

Distracting though the views undoubtedly are, 'High Moor' is not a place where anyone could safely spend a night in the open; even during the hours of daylight, the landscape is as grim and dangerous a prospect as any wilderness in the more remote parts of the Scottish Highlands. Not for nothing was it hailed as 'the National Park of Mordor' by Tolkien aficionado and chairman of the RAC, Sir Bertrand Vigours.

Sir Bertrand – a high-flying salary burner of no fixed dimensions, holder of several lucrative directorships and the kind of booming voice that always causes accidents in restaurants – never tired of recounting his own High Moor breakdown story to each new RAC 'Patrolman of the Year' at the company's annual dinner. No one who had heard his story ever drove across the moors alone again. By the time of his retirement, every single RAC rescue van covering the moor had a St Christopher's medal inset into the dashboard; a large, silver crucifix in the door tray; and a Gideon Bible in the glove compartment.

The patrolmen who were fortunate enough to enjoy a sober and serious Sir Bertrand at early doors also acquired different varieties of another item for self-protection that was certainly not included in the average breakdown mechanic's toolkit, but still sat very nicely in the palm of the hand or the square depression under the driver's seat.

Being as wild and unforgiving a place as could be conceived by an overactive imagination, High Moor had emerged in all it's terrifying glory from the Holocene period after the retreat of the same ice-age glaciers that had gouged out the fjords and inlets of Norway, and flattened every hill and knoll in Lincolnshire and Norfolk into a submissive sedimentary pulp.

The moor's true nature was only obvious from overhead, where its ankle-breaking topography, deadly sucking bogs and the crumbling brims of its many ravines were all too apparent. As if the sum of these plentiful dangers were not cruel enough, it had evolved a peculiar microclimate to rival the similarly daunting weather endured by Glencoe and Black Rannock Pass in Scotland. A micro climate that seemed to compress the brief seasons of spring and summer, yet extended the doldrums of autumn and winter with an almost conscious animal glee. To this day, it remains the most wild and remote part of North Yorkshire, and it is still a 'must do' for hikers and experienced fell runners, though every once in a while the moor 'does' for them. Bleak, featureless and barren, the bare chins of its hills were the first solid objects at height on the western side of the North Sea's storm-triangle coast. Trees, if they managed to survive at all past the size of a typical Bonsai, never grew past the height of a man. It was the ideal location for the Ministry of Defence's (MOD's) largest north-eastern radar station: Royal Air Force (RAF) Winderby. This location was the joint first most unpopular posting in the whole of the North Atlantic Treaty Organisation (NATO) along with Aird Ug on the Isle of Lewis, which still used its outside toilets as overspill for the cold store.

Winderby was the RAF's very own gulag of the damned: a punishment billet for those who had done something horrible or embarrassing, or horribly embarrassing, or scandalous and disgusting without technically earning an automatic discharge. A plaque in Latin – reading '*Vita est modo shit; ut in melius cum eo.*' – above the recreation room exit door summed up the miserable lot of its lifers: i.e. 'Your life is now shit; better get on with it.'

Unless playing chess, reading or photographing dramatic cloud formations was your favourite thing, there was very little else to do. The only other human beings within thirty miles were the owners of Craggy Farm in the pit of the Hole of Horcum and the staff of the Saltersgate Inn nearby, just beyond the caravan-wrecking bend known affectionately as 'Satan's Axle', where, once a day, a single bus arrived at the car park to pick up survivors.

The only living things on High Moor that actually seemed to enjoy their environment were the black-fleeced Henry Bond rams and ewes that made a living nibbling the young shoots of grass, which grew so vigorously around the fringes of the heather. Bond ram horns had evolved a 'firing forwards' position that no other breed had achieved, and, as a result, they cast a shadow that resembles a small, satanic Triceratops. The spiky prominence of Bond ram horns was a unique feature for an English breed, but it was as necessary for the rams' and ewes' peace of mind as the pistols and 'special' silver-tipped ammunition tucked under the seats of the RAC and AA breakdown trucks.

The Bonds' favourite grazing places were the tops of the ravines, on the borders of the heather and gorse, which made them all too easy to stumble upon by accident. The belligerent and territorial ewes were at least free of the deadly horns crowning the rams. A charging Bond could bayonet an unprotected leg or buttock to the depth of the Greater London edition of the *Yellow Pages*, then withdraw its horns and crunch their victim's hamstring faster than a hungry spaniel could gobble up a sausage roll – qualities that were usually enough to see off the less-determined members of the area's werewolf population, which were otherwise catered for by lame foxes, motor-vehicle breakdowns and amateur hikers. Or – if they were really, really lucky – a Weightwatchers' hiking party.

Chapter Two

Stopovers and Leg-Overs

In the relatively peaceful and prosperous decades since the end of the Second World War, High Moor's many hazards had been reinterpreted conscientiously by the crafty, hard-working copywriters of the North Yorkshire Moors Parks Authority (NYMPA) and the Yorkshire Tourist Board, as proof of its status as the 'last true wild wilderness of northern England', and promoted proudly throughout the English-speaking world as 'the Dartmoor of the north', minus the gaol and the nice ponies.

To their eternal credit, the Yorkshire race have always been an Olympic-standard breed when it comes to making a shilling out of a sow.

Several days after the dramatic 'Death and Destruction in Kettleness' headline in the *Whitby Gazette*, the nine members of the NYMPA's steering committee met for the first of their 'socials' – in the main bar of the Saltersgate Inn, which is close to the Hole of Horcum. This was in order, before the next high season, to float their best new ideas for the management of the park. The members attending their latest meeting were as follows:

Frank Boyes (chairman), chief executive officer (CEO) of
Mackenzie Dye Builders' Merchants Ltd (retired)

Trevor Roper (joint chairman), town clerk of Whitborough-on-Sea District Council (WBC)1968 – 80 (retired)

Joan Greene for The Ramblers' Association

Don Mears of the Royal Society for the Protection of Birds (RSPB)

Denise Featherstone of Ryedale District Council (RDC)

Dame Mary Vickers CBE of English Heritage

Richard Cole of *The Dalesman* magazine

Judith Clarke of Whitborough Historical Society

Malcolm Wood of Whitborough Historical Society

'Did everybody have a good Easter?' asked Frank, the committee's token local businessman, savouring his first sip of Pebbletrees' Owd Bob – Whitborough' s legendary lunatic brew.

'Aye. Can't complain, Frank,' replied Don.

'I see you've started on the strong stuff, Frank?' remarked Joan.

'It's safer than the Tetley's is around 'ere,' he muttered under his breath.

'Say again, Frank?' barked Joan as she fiddled and fumbled with her recalcitrant new hearing aid.

'Tetley's is off, Joan,' explained Don, looking cautiously at the landlord and his companion nearby at the bar – a sour-looking Detective Sergeant George Broadhead of Whitborough police.

'I hope that you're not driving home afterwards, Frank,' Joan continued, fidgeting with her cuffs.

'No, Joan, I thought I'd float back home,' said Frank, offering her his best sarcastic smile.

Joan enquired, 'Come again, Frank?'

'HE'S GOING HOME BY BOAT, JOAN,' boomed Richard.

'By *boat*? *Are you mad*? Just a minute,' she said soberly, 'you're having me on, aren't you? Dammit! This stupid thing in my ear is driving me mad. It's no good – I need to find a mirror.'

Frank and Trevor nodded sympathetically at their token ramblers' representative as Joan excused herself and strode off in search of a helpfully large mirror.

'So… what's happening in our usual room today? Has somebody booked it for a birthday party?' asked Trevor resentfully, nodding in the direction of the farthest annexe.

'It's some of your old lot, Trevor: it's a works party for the traffic wardens from the town hall,' remarked Judith. 'You want to go and have a look at the banner they've got up above the buffet in there – blummin' cheek!'

'Why? What does it say, Judith?' asked Mary.

'"Congratulations, Violet – 100 tickets in a week!" *That's what it says!* No wonder they've tried to hide it behind the nets. You should have a look at the food underneath the tablecloths in there too… paid for by us poor rate payers, no doubt. It's no surprise everyone an' his aunt who wants an easy life wants to work for the corporation,' said Judith indignantly.

'I'll tell you now, Judith,' said Trevor seriously, 'when I was in charge at the town hall, our wardens weren't on any sort of daft bonus scheme like they have now – and they were told to give everyone a bit of leeway or the benefit of the doubt. That's why they never had to worry about getting punched or screamed at. We had proper standards in my day.'

'It's a damn liberty, if you ask me. Gloating like that behind closed doors about your hundredth weekly ticket,' said Richard, before his attention wandered again. 'I see we've got that bikers' club, the Vikings, in the upstairs suite today too,' he said, noticing the passage of a huge, bearded man wearing a leather waistcoat that was held together with rally patches.

'Wardens and bikers, what a mix,' muttered Don.

'I won't hear a word said about those lads from the Vikings Motorcycle Club [MCC] from you, Don Mears,' said Judith. 'They're very nice indeed, I'll have you know! Some of them are the best people we've ever had in the historical society. Just because they look a bit rough doesn't mean they're mean too; you couldn't wish to meet a kindlier bunch of lads. They mek a *lovely* cup of tea,' she cooed, closing her eyes with a blissful squeeze.

'I'd vouch for 'em too, Jude. A cleverer bunch o' lads you'd never meet,' added Malcolm – the historical society's best trench troll – as his opening contribution to the debate. 'The Vikings got an MA, two MSc's a GBH, an ABH and three TWOCs, so one o' their lasses said.'

'What's a TWOC, Malcolm? I haven't heard of that qualification before,' asked Richard.

'It's like a City and Guilds in vehicle maintenance. You have to do two years for it, apparently,' confirmed Malcolm.

The other committee members, who had all led very sheltered lives, contemplated their drinks and made approving bovine noises. At the bar, Detective Sergeant Broadhead and his friend, the landlord, were almost choking on their beers.

'Well, it looks like I stand corrected,' replied Don sarcastically, 'it's a good job Mad Mel H over in Whitborough doesn't know about tonight's social, eh Jude? Or we'd have a party of gatecrashers armed with pickaxe handles.'

'Mel who?' asked Joan.

'Mel Hazard – one of Whitborough's untouchables. He's one of the Whitborough mafia, Joan. He owns Costigans' Amusement Arcade, Silverado's, the Tunny Club and the chippy on Landkey Island. Mad Mel must have got more parking tickets down the years than we've had hot dinners. I swear to God he's never paid any of 'em. He hates wardens more than he hates the revenue. He even tried to run one of 'em down in his Porsche once,' explained Don.

'He's got a GBH an' all,' said Broadhead sarcastically, just within range of the committee's hearing. If any of them heard his contribution, they let it pass. Their host, the landlord, who was unable to control his own imminent eruption of laughter, dashed off to the men's to smother his howls of mirth with a beer towel.

'Do the police know about that?' asked Trevor disapprovingly.

'You'd have to be brave or daft to shop Mad Mel. Though I very much doubt he meant to run anyone down…' said Judith.

'How do you know that, Judith?' asked Trevor mystified.

She answered sheepishly, 'My sister used to clean for him.'

'Oh well…That settles it then – innocent of all charges,' scoffed Trevor.

'Are you being sarcastic, Trevor?' asked Judith.

Frank enquired, 'In a Porsche you say, Don?', as he was trying to deflect Judith's ire to take the heat off his deputy.

'Aye. That great big, white thing with the matching bodykit.'

9

'Oh, how *vulgar*,' griped Mary.

'Shame it wasn't a Jaguar,' said Richard. 'I don't know why more people who've got a bit of cash don't buy British.'

'I don't think this is a matter for levity,' replied Trevor sternly.

'Quite right, Trevor. Right, people, let's stay on topic shall we?' added Frank, trying to steer the conversation around to the agenda, though the majority of his colleagues seemed to be more interested in speculating on what kind of buffet food they were going to be watching the partying traffic wardens eat.

'Have you seen those four great speakers behind the microphone stand in our room? It looks like those wardens have booked a band and a DJ too,' moaned Judith.

'A band, Jude?'

'Aye. Roland or something,' Judith explained,' Their name's on that big, black keyboard.'

'Roland? What kind of daft name is that for a band?' smirked Richard.

'That's nothing, Richard; you'll never guess the name of my daughter's favourite band,' said Don.

'What?' Richard queried.

'Orchestral Manoeuvres in the Dark…'he said, as if announcing the defection of Geoff Boycott to Lancashire County Cricket Club.

'Orchestral Manoeuvres in the Dark?'

'Aye. As I live and breathe…'

'Our eldest, Marcus, is obsessed with some louts called Spear of Desk Tidy[1] and the Sisters of Mercy,' muttered

---

1   Or, as they are known in the real world, Spear of Destiny.

Denise despairingly, '*The Sisters of Mercy*! If you could see what he's done to his hair! He looks like one of those toy gonks.'

'Teenagers, eh…Who'd 'ave 'em?' Sighed Malcolm, more to himself, than anyone else.

'Would anyone like to start us off on park business?' asked Frank hopefully.

'What are we banning this year?' asked Joan, taking her seat as the proud new owner of a properly positioned hearing aid.

'Skateboarding,' said Frank and Trevor, chortling in perfect unison.

'Skateboarding?'

'Aye. *Skateboarding*. In the car parks… Richard knows all about it; don't you, Richard?' enquired Frank.

'Aye. Best to get to grips with it now, before it gets out of hand.'

'Teenagers!' grumbled Malcolm, ignoring everything and everybody except the head on his beer.

'Would you like to contribute something, Malcolm?' asked Mary.

'Nahh, I'll just sit this one out thanks, Maz.'

'My name, *Malcolm*, is *Mary*. I am not a "*Maz*"! Is there a problem with people skateboarding in the car parks, Trevor?' asked Mary with icy precision, once she'd put Malcolm in his place for his over familiarity.

'Well, maybe not yet so much, but that's not the point. It's dangerous, int' it. Kids on wheels… swerving about. *Showing off…*'

'Aye, bad business… people showing off. Showing off's bad for tourism.'

'We can't 'ave people enjoying their sens. They need to remember where they are…'

'And where are they, Don?' asked Mary.

'They're in Yorkshire. We don't want any o' that enjoying yerself nonsense in Yorkshire. It upsets the sparrowhawks. Meks the grouse sterile– *well known.*'

'And what do you propose to remedy that, just out of interest, Don?' asked Denise.

'Well, I'm glad you asked me that, Denise,' replied Don, thinking the exact opposite. 'Er… it's er…'

'Difficult to say?' interjected Mary unhelpfully.

'I think what Don's trying to say is we need to manage our visitor numbers carefully during the peak season. Isn't that right, Don?' stated Frank diplomatically.

'That's exactly what I was about to say, Frank; thank you,'

'So that would include little girls and boys roller skating, would it? *And* kids on buggies? Just so we're clear,' said Denise.

'Aye. Damn right it would! There's nowt so dangerous as a three-year-old slamming into yer ankles in a cart wi' no brakes when you're holding a hot flask o' tea! People die of less…'ranted Don.

'And *what else* would you'd like to ban?' asked Joan tetchily. 'That's not actually become an issue yet…'

'Folk look to people like us to ban stuff before it starts getting popular. That's the point, Joan,' said Richard.

'I'm not convinced it's a problem, Richard,' interjected Mary. 'We haven't had a single complaint about roller skating or skateboarders to date – am I correct?'

'And what about hang gliding? We should definitely ban hang gliding…far too dangerous,' said Don, agitating on behalf of the grouse and the sparrowhawks.

'Don, hang-gliders can't take off on the moor, and they certainly can't run up and down the road trying to take off,' said Richard.

'No, they wouldn't dare, cos the bloody werewolves would ave' em,' muttered the landlord at the bar, just within earshot of the committee members. His comment seemed to guillotine what little conversational spirit there was across the tables ringing the bar, replacing an atmosphere of comfortable boredom with a sudden alert silence that waited impatiently upon his next words, but his next utterance was only to ask whether Mr and Mrs Farrar at table three wanted tartar sauce or tomato ketchup with their haddock and chips.

'What did he just say?' whispered Judith, leaning towards her female colleagues opposite.

'Werewolves… huh! No surprise to most of us; the moor's always had 'em,' said Richard matter-of-factly. Trevor, Frank and Don grunted in agreement.

'I'm sorry, but why are we going from the silly to the downright ridiculous? Shall we all just come down from our little flights of fancy?' protested Mary.

'We could ban 'em from landing,' said Trevor, 'What do you think, Frank?'

'What – the werewolves?'

'The ruddy hang-gliders, Don!' snapped Trevor.

'Why on earth would these hang-gliders want to land out there anyway?' asked Denise, genuinely perplexed.

'They might need to land for a pee,' said Don.

'*Land for a pee!* Are you mental, Don?' Said Judith.

'Just a hang on a minute, please. can we all just rewind a moment to discuss what Richard was alluding to…What do you mean "werewolves", Richard?' asked Denise.

'Before we go off on a tangent, could someone explain how these hang-glider pilots are going to see our "No hang-gliders" signs from up there?' Said Joan, jabbing an arthritic forefinger towards the ceiling.

'Well, we can put it to a vote when we meet next week proper.'

'Richard, what do you mean by "werewolves"?'snapped Denise.

'What do I mean by "werewolves", Denise?'

'*Yes!*'

'Well it's not a word that's open to misinterpretation, is it?'

'But you're not serious, surely?' she almost spluttered.

'Well, why don't you ask the landlord, Denise – he's right behind you?' replied Richard.

'I have every intention of doing just that. Very soon,' she replied adroitly. Absolutely determined that she was not going to do anything of the sort.

'That's George Broadhead of Whitborough police,' said Frank, nodding to George at the bar. 'He's one of our better coppers. Can we just drop the werewolves for the moment and concentrate on the hang-gliders?' asked Frank irritably.

'Perhaps you could ask those nice people who run the base at Winderby if they would be so kind as to shoot them down for us when they stray over the park?' added Joan helpfully, 'Just to make sure.'

'Well, there must be something else we can ban,' suggested Trevor, as a man who'd had a whole twelve years' experience of hearing motions to ban things as a town clerk. 'What about a ban on caravans and motor homes parking overnight?'

'That could fly, Trevor…'mused Frank, winking at his deputy.

'No stopovers for leg-overs,' added the RSPB's man in the room.

'I beg your pardon, Don?' fumed Mary. 'Do you mind?'

'Sorry, Mary; I'm just trying to lighten the atmosphere,' replied Don sheepishly.

'Please don't be crude,'

'Sorry, Mary.'

'This whole meeting is degenerating into an unseemly grudge match of obscene bickering.'

'Teenagers, eh…Who'd 'ave 'em?'

'OH, SHUT UP, MALCOLM!' shouted Joan, Judith and Mary in unison.

'We could fine people for littering; that'll bring some money in,' suggested Richard.

'We already fine people for littering, Richard,' said Frank. 'How much did that bring in last year, Trevor?'

'Not even a hundred quid,' said Trevor. 'Ask Joan how much rubbish her members pick up on their travels… Joan?'

'My hearing is fine now, thank you, Trevor. The answer to your question, Richard, is not enough to take a bag on a regular basis,' she confirmed.

'We have to rely on the public to report people dumping their rubbish,' said Frank.

'Oh, but aren't the wardens supposed to police that?'

'They will – if they're around to see it. But they can't be everywhere at once. We only fund four,' explained Frank.

'So, it's the Status Quo then…' said Richard, 'Denim all round.'

His colleagues looked at him strangely and then, suddenly, the plectrum dropped.

'Well, if we're going to refuse to talk about your werewolves, Richard, I think we should talk about a motion to ban high-powered cars and motorcycles,' said Denise for the ladies.

'Good luck with that…'scoffed Don.

'I'm serious. They're dangerous, Don.'

'The whole damn park's dangerous, Denise,' said Trevor. 'It's the only reason most of the tourists are coming here in the first place. The more you try to mollycoddle folk, the more they'll look for excitement.'

'Why would you say something like that?'Denise queried.

'Why? Because it's true. Dangerous hobbies are also *exciting*. That's why people climb mountains and wrestle crocodiles. You can't wrap people up in cotton wool their whole lives – they just get bored.'

'That must be why the Aussies are so hard to beat,' grumbled Malcolm, lamenting the result of the last test match.

'May I make a suggestion, please? Instead of all this talk of banning things and fining people, why don't we bring a few new activities into the park that people might enjoy and can *really* get behind?' suggested Mary.

'Like stopovers and leg-overs?' asked Don.

'Right… I've had quite enough of your filth, Don Mears. It was nice to see you all again,' said Mary curtly, 'but I'm going home. I thought I was coming to a relaxing pre-committee meeting, but this is obviously something *quite different*.'

'Don, I think you should apologise to Mary.' Said Frank.

'Sorry, Mary,' said Don sheepishly.

'Don't say it unless you mean it, Don. And smirking is hardly an admittance of contrition,' scolded Mary, buttoning up her jacket.

Their RSPB colleague did indeed carry a permanent air of impish merriment, and so he had to be careful not to put himself in situations where it might be misinterpreted. But his default expression had more to do with having a naturally friendly countenance and spending too much time squinting through a pair of binoculars.

'No, thank you all for the concern, but I'll not stay today I think, 'continued Mary briskly, 'I'm not going to sit here – on this committee – as the comic foil of a filthy-minded avian fetishist like you Don Mears. Goodbye, everyone.'

'Watch out for them werewolves on your way home, Mary,' said Malcolm.

Chapter Three

The Diddytastic Punch-Up and the Ten Geese of the Apocalypse

Detective Sergeant George Broadhead followed the departure of Dame Mary Vickers with a covert eye from his favoured perch at the end of the long bar in the Saltersgate Inn, and he wondered whether the NYMPA committee meeting was about to break up, just as it was beginning to get interesting. Luckily for him, the other committee members didn't appear to want to follow her out, and he sensed that there was a good chance they might revive their fascinating conversation so he could continue to eavesdrop and pick up some interesting titbits for his mental archive. Broadhead, the slightly younger half of Whitborough's most successful crime-fighting duo, began to relax a little more and let his eyes drift over the sweep of the lounge whilst taking a fresh mouthful of beer. The inn's long bar was a fine place to sit and contemplate those cases that stubbornly refused to be solved, far away from the distracting demands of his uptight superiors. It was even more valuable as a breathing space now that he was also having to contend with the sinister presence of overseers from the Home Office and the MOD – whose underlying motivations he was beginning to question. At least two of these guests were revealing a most unethical interest in identifying promising scapegoats, even as they were pretending to assist his team in finding the perpetrators of the Easter-weekend terrorism. His rather blunt appraisal of his predicament was not yet something he was willing to broadcast in professional company, so he had decided to do the next best thing and let out some of his frustrations over a pint with his favourite publican.

Broadhead was almost at the bottom of his first drink and was contemplating having a second before setting off back to Whitborough, following a visit to Whitby Hospital for a chat with Police Constable (PC) Jackson Alger. Eavesdropping on the NYMPA committee meeting had proved unexpectedly rewarding, even if he might have to warn his superiors that his host and some of the more distinguished guests at the Saltersgate Inn thought the moors were overrun by terrifying supernatural predators with huge fangs. It wasn't the first time that week he had heard somebody talking about werewolves, as though they were actually flesh and blood. There was something unpleasant building in the borough, and Broadhead's radar was on red alert.

'You having another one, George?' asked the landlord.

'Aye, why not?' George decided. 'They can stew without me at the station for a bit longer. It's quite remarkable what you overhear in the right sort of pub.'

'I'll take that as a compliment, shall I?'

'Don't worry, Pat. I'm not about to break cover in here.'

'Well, that's reassuring. I bet your lot in Whitborough have had their hands full since that ship blew up.'

'Huh! You wouldn't believe all the extra company we've had lately. We could get a lot more done if we weren't having our every move monitored by the MOD and the thugs from the Home Office. And they're just the ones I can tell *you* about.'

'Well, I've got a party of traffic wardens in later. Not that they compare to the company you're keeping. One of 'em is celebrating her hundredth weekly ticket, so I put 'em in the annexe for their own good. If any of my regulars knew I had a copper in here *and* a party of traffic wardens on the same afternoon, I'd probably be empty for the rest of the year. No offence…'

'Very wise, putting the parking gestapo out of sight in the other room.'

'We've got a right house full today. The wardens, the Vikings MCC, that lot there from the NYMPA committee and then the Ken Dodd fan club too. They should be here any minute.'

'Ken Dodd's fan club?'

'Yep. They visit every pub and hotel Ken stays in. Old Doddy got trapped here once in a snow storm on the way to a gig at Newcastle Mayfair. It's a good job he found this place before… well…the moor's not a Diddytastic place to break down, it must be said.'

'You don't seriously believe there're werewolves out there do you?'

'Come on, George… you must have heard the stories. You know all the AA and RAC patrolmen are packing when they drive through here don't you? And don't use that little titbit against them or you'll find no one wants to share your company… agreed?'

Broadhead nodded sulkily.

'You must have heard about what happened to Slade and Showaddywaddy when they stopped for a jimmy near the base years ago,' declared the landlord. 'There've been no tour buses coming across this moor again since. We used to have all the big names stopping here until those bloody things started showing up: Sandie Shaw and Cliff Richard, and we even had the Everly Brothers using the loo out the back.'

'Why on earth would they come through here?' asked George.

'They wanted to taste some proper Yorkshire fish 'n' chips and see a bit o' the countryside. The A1's fast, but it ain't very scenic, is it?'

'D'you mind if I scribble something down for a minute? 'requested Broadhead, taking out his notepad.

'You've got ten minutes before me Diddy-army arrive. Just give me a second to take Barbara Taylor Bradford out of the video player and put Ken in. If I have to watch *A Woman of* bloody *Substance* again this week - or the ruddy *Thorn Birds* – I'm gonna vault this bar and brain someone,' the landlord grumbled, alluding to his wife's favourite TV programmes.

★

The Diddy-brawl wasn't the first big fight at the Saltersgate Inn, but it was certainly one of the most expensive. The last one involving the forces of law and order happened one lunchtime in the harsh winter of 1947, when two working parties of prisoners of war (POWs) from Eden camp near Malton – one German and one Italian – arrived to clear the snow drifts that had almost buried the roadside hedges. The Italians, already fed up with the cold, downed their shovels when they found out that the Germans had stolen a carrot and two coal 'eyes' from 'Frederrico', their snowman, and a huge snowball fight had ensued, which was only stopped by an AA patrolman who drove his motorbike and sidecar at the ringleaders in the car park to frustrate their anger, whilst kicking their shins with his boots. Thirty-six years later, it took just one pair of bruised knees to cause the biggest brawl ever.

The pick-up of the traffic wardens' awards party from Whitborough got off to a bad start when their star attraction, Violet, insisted on travelling alone – except for the driver – on the front seat of their minibus, because of her mini skirt. Karen Metcalfe, who had already assumed she would have possession of the front bench seat on account of her size, was forced to squeeze into a pair of single seats behind, where her ample knees were forced to endure thirty miles of bumps and knocks until she reached the Saltersgate Inn in a mood to kill.

By the time they'd reached the inn, she was unable to remove her mack because it was the only thing covering the giant, purple bruises on her knees, which she'd acquired during the drive. The first thing she did when the party disembarked was to find the pub's payphone and call her sister Val, Whitborough's legendary 'lady' doorman, to ask her to come and pick her up in her Ford Cortina.

Whilst her work colleagues sat talking in the annexe and watching the DJ connect his last few cables, Violet was having a ball parading her slim physique and fabulous derriere around the main bar, with the confidence of a woman still on the right side of drunk. The impossibly handsome Flight Sergeant Alan Whyte of RAF Winderby had caught her eye, and she was doing her very best to get his attention. Meanwhile, Ken Davis – the council's manager in charge of parking, parks and gardens – was trying to avoid the rebellious atmosphere brewing amongst his wardens in the annexe by ferrying boxes of party streamers and the runner-up prizes from the back of the minibus. It wasn't too long before he got his first complaint…

'Ken – can we start on the food now?' asked Karen, pointing at the newly uncovered buffet. 'Some of us are bloody starving!'

'I suppose so. Where's Vi?'

'Huh! She's abandoned us already…She's parading around and flaunting her assets in the main bar.'

'She's not drunk, is she?'

'I've no idea. I couldn't care less.'

'Karen, this is a real milestone for our team. I'm not going to stand for any animosity tonight.'

'Shall I go and fetch her, Ken? Perhaps she doesn't know we're nearly ready?' asked their most shy and retiring colleague, Mr Barraclough.

'She knows we're ready,' retorted Karen sarcastically.

'She isn't here with us in the annex yet, Karen, because I asked her specifically to wait near the bar so I could unwrap her surprise,' confirmed Ken.

'What, a male stripper?'

'Somebody trod on your foot, have they?' sneered Colin, Karen's other arch-enemy.

'Watch it, Colin!'

'Why? What are you gonna do – sit on me?'

'*What did you call me?*' stormed Karen.

'JUST SHUT UP THE PAIR OF YOU! Or you can all get right back in that bloody minibus!' yelled Ken.

'I'm not staying *here* all night,' grunted Karen.

'What's that?'

'I'M GOING HOME.'

'Oh, why? Are you ill, Karen?'

'Am I ill? My bloody knees look like a bluebottle's arse from sitting in the back of that minibus, squeezed up against the front seat. I'll be sending you a sick note for next week. I'll have to stay indoors until these bloody bruises disappear; you do realise that, do you? *Just look at me legs!*' she moaned loudly, flashing a pair of fleshy knees covered in dark-purple bruises. '*I'm black and blue!*'

'*Oh!* Oh dear…' said Ken.

'I DON'T WANT YOUR DAMN SYMPATHY. I WANT TO GO HOME! So you can take me off the bloody rota first thing tomorrow morning.'

*

Outside the inn, the Ken Dodd fan club had arrived from Leeds finally in their modified Diddy-mobile: a Plaxton's coach with tickling-stick pattern seat covers and a huge set of plastic teeth on the coach's front grille. It took the party a whole ten minutes to disembark, on account of their gigantic, oversized shoes and hats, but the doors closed eventually, and the driver settled down for a nap whilst a great Diddy-crowd of Diddymen, Diddywomen, and Diddyboys and Diddygirls negotiated the inn's front steps and double-door sets in their great Diddy-shoes.

Whilst her manager dashed back and forth, Karen Metcalfe felt free to sow more discord and dissatisfaction amongst the wardens who were already resenting Violet's' disrespectful' absence and were starting to mutter amongst themselves in-between trips to the finger buffet. Karen, the council's shit-stirrer par excellence, was getting into her stride, but not all of her colleagues were so ready to sympathise with her constant grumbling and negativity. At least half of them were more than ready to give her a taste of her own medicine.

'I've told Ken already. I said I'll not be staying late me. My sister's picking me up at soon,' declared Karen.

'Oh…Oh well, more food for the rest of us.'

'I beg your pardon, Dominic. What are you inferring?'

'I'm not implying anything, Karen. I'm just stating the obvious.'

'Yes, you did! *YOU* just inferred I was fat!'

'No, I didn't.'

'Yes, you did!'

'No, I didn't.'

'Dominic did not say you were fat, Karen,' said Violet's friend Paula.

'Where's your best mate Violet, Paula…Are we not good enough company anymore?'

'She's in the loo.'

'Draped around the neck of some bloke more like.'

'Well at least she looks after herself, Karen,' retorted Paula.

'If anyone else calls me fat, I'm gonna flatten 'em. Right?'

'Karen, calm down. You're making a right scene of yourself.'

'Don't you dare tell me to calm down Paula Skinny Arse!'

'She means spectacle, Karen.'

'I know what I mean, Dominic,' said Paula acidly, 'just like Fat Arse does.'

'What did you call me!' yelled Karen, just before their DJ's first announcement finally tipped her over the edge.

'Here's one for all you bigger girls and larger ladies out there tonight. It's Queen with "Fat Bottomed Girrrls",' purred Bruce Butcher, as his lighting rig and junction boxes came to life; followed swiftly by Karen Metcalfe's long dormant tantrum, which involved a flying ashtray, a full plate of sandwiches and a Saltersgate Inn bar stool.

★

At the very same moment that Karen Metcalfe began hurling plates, and the pub's loose fixtures and fittings, Whitborough's most ruthless traffic warden and witch bumped into a close relative of one of her less satisfied 'customers' in the hall at the foot of the staircase.

'I KNOW YOU; you're that woman that made my sister cry on the Fish Quay!'

'Pardon me? Who the bloody hell are you?' slurred Violet.

'I'm her brother, *madam*. And you're that horrible, ticket-mad traffic warden from Whitborough, aren't you?'

'And who are you... dressed up like Coco the bleeding clown?'

'I'm not a *clown*. I'm the Diddy-king of Knotty Ash...'

'Well, you can get knotted,' slurred Violet, sticking two purple-painted fingernails in the direction of the Ken Dodd fan club's handiest Diddy. 'Go and Diddy-stuff yourself.'

Had Violet been sober, the next few minutes would have been a lot less expensive and painful for all involved. But the only uncertainty of hurling an insult at a native of Knotty Ash when they already have a serious grievance against you is how long their fist is going to take to reach your chin. And so it was for the daddy of Diddies – 'Big Daddy' Desi Vaughan

– who went straight for Violet's slender neck with his Diddy-great fingers.

The pair stumbled backwards until they bashed into the hall table, scattering the inn's brochure display, the cutlery trays, a Dartington crystal vase of yellow tulips, a rare Haliburton telephone and an irreplaceable William Morris hat-and-coat stand; all of which occurred at the same moment Karen Metcalfe's stool hit the warden's guest DJ square in the face as he was priming their next record.

As the two mismatched wrestlers began their slow fall towards the floor, Violet managed to push her left palm between her face and the wobbly press of her attacker's bulbous nose, as she hit the carpet on top of eighteen stones of furious Diddy.

Fortunately, her free hand found one of the fish forks from the floor, which she used to stab her jauntily dressed attacker hard in the armpit – now that their fall had knocked the air out of her assailant and loosened his grip from her throat. She stabbed it hard again into the side of his belly, forcing his head up into the arc of a viciously swung bed-warmer, as he screamed for mercy with all the power in his great Diddy lungs. Ken, her manager and saviour, completed a perfectly timed double knockout by felling the landlord, who had steamed into the hall at just the right moment to catch the bed-warmer on its backswing. Ken Davis had never picked up a bed-warmer in his life before he saw Violet being strangled, though he clearly had the makings of an excellent batsman. He was just examining his first two corpses and the two face-shaped depressions in the head of the copper pan when the Vikings rushed down the stairs ready for war, with their pool cues and bullet belts swinging, just as the wardens fled the function room and the rain of flying china from Karen Metcalfe's plate storm.

Ken looked at his two prone victims once more before locking eyes with the first biker to reach the bottom of the stairs, ran into the men's, and locked himself in one of the cubicles. Violet was just pushing herself up on her elbows when Karen Metcalfe stormed out of the function room, knocked over two of her colleagues, then tripped over Ken's unconscious Diddy and crashed into the first biker at the bottom of the stairs, pulling down his jeans. Then the man lost his balance, fell over Karen and head butted Paula, Violet's friend. Violet stabbed him in the bottom with a fish knife and threw another at the head of the next biker on the stairs.

More bodies poured into the hall from the adjoining rooms to add to the sudden press of bikers. Then all hell broke loose as the right flank of the Diddy front line panicked, and made a grab for the ceremonial knot of pikestaffs, claymores and axes mounted on the wall. The traffic wardens, fearing the worst, snatched up whatever cutlery they could find and dashed forwards in a chaotic charge, provoking the Vikings and Diddy men to violence when they were only looking for a quick way out of the brawl. Violet, now crouching behind a small hostess trolley, decided to retreat in the interests of self-preservation and crawled back to safety along the skirting on her hands and knees, just missing George Broadhead's sudden downfall, courtesy of a forehead-cracking claymore pommel.

The Diddy boys and Diddy girls whose parents were disgracing themselves in a mass brawl rushed out of the pub and banged on the doors of their coach demanding to be let on board, whilst the seven terrified members of the NYMPA committee fled into the conservatory or back to their cars.

The landlord's call to Whitborough police for emergency assistance before his concussion – prompt and timely as it was – could not stop the re-enactment of the Battle of Stirling Bridge that was being refought in the hall. But it did at least mean that the losers and the wounded would be arrested promptly and processed with all the care and sympathy that the force was so renowned for. But, on this particular occasion, they would be doing a lot more stretcher carrying than reading of rights.

Eventually, Violet managed to crawl out of the melee she had started and staggered clumsily through rear ranks of the Knotty Ash reserve to the safety of the hall doors. Emerging into an apparently deserted lounge bar in a torn dress and one stiletto short, she looked around hastily for a weapon to upgrade her bloodstained fish fork, then caught sight of the gorgeous, male stranger in RAF blues, who was facing the window. After tearing her black dress a little closer to the edge of her bra, she fluffed up her hair, tottered theatrically to the back of his chair and fell backwards into the lap of the gorgeously handsome Flight Sergeant Whyte, who was completely oblivious to the skirmish unfolding behind him, being cosseted under the humming earphones of his Sony Walkman. Alan had been enjoying his *Best of Queen* cassette, unlike the fat-bottomed girl a few doors away, who had given up trying to make the rocking world go round and was back in the annexe, making the most of the empty room by filling her carrier bag with smoked salmon tartlets – once she had got rid of the last of her anger by kicking over the DJ's speakers with her pumps.

'WHAT ARE YOU DOING?' yelped Whyte, pulling out his headphones.

'Oh, love! You've got to get me out of here,' gasped Violet, craftily manipulating the direction of her rescuer's gaze by pulling her bra strap back into place.

'What's happened to you?' asked Flight Sergeant Whyte, once he'd got over the shock of having a rather attractive, though dishevelled, older female fall into his lap. 'Have you been raped, miss?'

'My name's Violet, pet; just get me out of here. Where's your car?'

'Outside, but it's—'

'I don't care if it's your mum's; just get me the hell out of here!'

'It is *not* my mother's. I'm a flight sergeant in the RAF… *is there some kind of fight in the hall?*' he said, suddenly alert to the barrage of cries, screams and smashing plates beyond the hall doors.

'It's not a fight, pet; it's a bloody massacre. Come on, you'll have to pick me up.'

'Pick you…?'

'YES…PICK ME UP. YOU KNOW, WITH YOUR ARMS! YOU'RE A BLOODY PILOT AREN'T YOU?'

'No, but—'

'No, but what? I've lost my shoes; I can't walk on gravel in me tights!'

'*Oh!*'

'"Oh" indeed. Well, what are you waiting for?'

'Let's get you outside first, shall we?' suggested Alan tentatively, struck dumb by Violet's forcefulness – and her fabulously trim figure. 'Do you think you could let go of that fork with the all the blood on it, miss?'

★

Back in the corridor, the candy-coloured Diddy-mob were in fighting retreat, trying to keep their balance in their oversized shoes, as the bikers got over their initial shyness about battering the life-sized equivalents of one of their childhood icons, who had been trying to keep them at bay with the pub's display swords and pikestaffs. Although the landlord's weapons display was not being brandished with any genuine harmful intent, the Diddy men could not have known that waving a blade or an axe in the faces of the Vikings was the equivalent of a declaration of war. As the pool cues flew and the bullet belts chopped down, the Diddy men panicked again, throwing away their blades and axes, but doing so in a manner guaranteed to be misinterpreted as aggression by the gang of big, hairy men who were travelling down the angry slope to drunk. The bikers' girlfriends, by contrast, remained upstairs, unconcerned with the mayhem below and confident in their men folk's ability to come out on top in any game of fists. Kirsty Brakes dealt her friends another hand of cards and finished off her absent boyfriend's pint of Merrydoome cider, whilst he dragged the brim of a Knotty Ash dress hat past the eyes and ears of his opponent, bent him over, and threw him into the buckets-and-mops cupboard.

'How long d'you reckon it'll be before the cops get here, Kirst? Did you get through to the station?' asked Tracey.

'About twenny minutes, they said. Somebody else called 'em from 'ere too. Sounds like our lads are winning again though.'

'Who are those stoopid psychos in the funny suits and the daft hats?'

'The Ken Dodd fan club. S'what it said on the coach.'

'I hate clowns.'

'They're not clowns, Trace – they're Diddy men.'

'Diddy-what?'

'Diddy men!'

'Have they got small dicks or summat?'

'Trace, didn't you have a TV when you was growing up?'

'Nope, our old man sold it for two' undred quid's worth of fags with us carpets…He's not our bloody problem n'more though: the rotten old swine died years ago. It were a bad pie at Glastonbury. Me mum used to say it were "pietic" justice. He were a nasty piece of work my old man…He sold me Raleigh tricycle for a can o' Special Brew. Basterd.'

There was a horrible scream from below as one of the bikers gained possession of a pikestaff and thrust the barely blunted front spike into the gonads of the last fish-knife-hurling Diddy.

'*Oooh'eck!* Someone's got a bullseye,' she cackled. 'Shall we go check on the lads?'

'*Naah.* They'll be reet,' said Kirsty proudly, 'They'll be done in a minute, then we can wrap up this crap game before the cops arrive.'

★

Moments later, the last Diddy standing went down screaming under the vicious swat of a bullet belt, but there was one last comeuppance due before the fighting stopped – and the ten geese of the apocalypse were on their way to deliver it.

A scrum of attacking geese is a terrifying thing. The unbearable volume of their battle cry – an unendurable honking screech – could blot out the noise of a Parisian traffic jam. In a massed attack, they are vicious, relentless, impossible to stop and impossible to escape. They are the guard dogs of choice in the countryside, and the Saltersgate Inn had ten of them. Don Mears knew the pub's birds were the NYMPA committee's best chance of survival, once he had glimpsed the full horror of the battle unfolding in the hall, and he was very keen it didn't spread into the conservatory, where he and his colleagues were crouching under the window sills. With the same low cunning he used to counter poachers and egg collectors, he set about shepherding the landlord's honking bodyguards from the yard, through the conservatory and into the short bridging passage between him, his fellow committee members, and the bikers and Diddy men. He craftily set fire to a metal waste-paper bin filled with beer mats, which he used to chase the birds in the direction of the brawl and antagonise them enough to turn them into a malevolent, feathered blitzkrieg of honking, homicidal fury.

Once the tidal wave of white-feathered death joined the fray – screeching, snapping and tearing at the unprotected noses, fingers and earlobes of the Vikings – the bikers turned and fled, with their leather jackets pulled over their heads, battered by wings and gouged by ferocious beaks, dropping their helmets, tripping over rugs and bouncing off the furniture as they tumbled out of the exits as fast as their feet could carry them. Only one had failed to make the exit when a flapping wing broke his wrist, and so he ran for the safety of the telephone box in the bar to hide from the hissing birds. Their girlfriends, still trapped upstairs, used the old hayloft door to the fire escape to join their men folk, going in a wide circle around the perimeter to the front car park to avoid the angry geese. The rest of the flock only began to back off when the bikers started their machines and redlined their engines to deter the birds from making another assault, before roaring off towards Pickering, just as Violet launched herself at her rescuer, Flight Sergeant Whyte, from the passenger seat of his Land Rover.

★

Val Metcalfe, Whitborough's infamous door security 'lady', was not best pleased to be buzzed by a squadron of speeding Japanese superbikes so soon after turning right in her Cortina at the Fox and Rabbit pub, a few miles south of the Saltersgate Inn. She resisted the temptation to shake her fist at the onslaught in favour of keeping both hands on the wheel and her Cortina on a straight track, but she did allow herself a few choice expletives as their machines rushed past her door panel with inches to spare in a howl of revs. They were swiftly followed by a swarm of screaming two-stroke machines speeding towards her like a gang of huge, metal wasps, coming perilously close to slicing off her driver's side mirror and leaving several mysterious white feathers stuck in its seams. By the time she drew up in the Saltersgate Inn's car park, she was as red faced as a marathon runner and in the mood for a fight, but less ignorant of where the feathers had come from. Val extracted herself from her Cortina, stomped towards the doors of the inn and strode purposefully through the main bar to find her sister. Then she heard the sound of distant police sirens.

The scene inside the pub was as bizarre and ugly as anything she'd seen in a lifetime of war films and door work. A gaggle of geese were honking and fighting over scraps of leather; the furniture was in disarray; axes, swords and

34

abandoned pikestaffs covered the floors; and blood-spatter patterns covered the architraves and carpets, then Detective Sergeant Broadhead stumbled through the hall doors, clutching a bloody bullet belt with the clear and distinct imprint of a sword pommel in the middle of his forehead.

'Bleedin' 'ell, George! What the friggin' 'ell happened in 'ere?' asked Val.

'A Diddy tastic f**king punch-up – that's what,' he mumbled, before dropping the bullet belt and throwing up onto the Space Invaders console.

★

Violet's misreading of her gallant rescuer's intentions came down to two small things: the post hormonal rush of her dramatic escape from the brawl, and the three rum and Cokes she'd drunk after finishing off a bottle of champagne in Whitborough. Consequently, Flight Sergeant Whyte's consent hadn't even come into the equation. Trapped in his seat, with Violet's lips clamped over his mouth and her scampering hands in all sorts of personal places, he accidentally disengaged his door handle in his panic and suddenly found himself toppling sideways out of his Land Rover with a sex-mad traffic warden clamped to his neck. Fortunately, one of the policeman from Pickering saw his plight and arrived in the nick of time to push him back onto his seat; Whyte's coarse and ungrateful response wasn't quite what the young constable was expecting.

'Oooh, pet – you've got *lovely* smooth skin, 'cried Violet, sticking her tongue in the flight sergeant's ear.

'Get this crazy bitch off me!'

'Sir, are you in a relationship with this lady?' asked the constable.

'No, I am *not* in a relationship with this *lady*; she asked me to help her outside, then she tried to tear my bloody uniform off me in my Land Rover. She's as drunk as a bloody skunk!' explained Whyte.

'You ungrateful twat!' cried Violet. 'You don't know what you're missing. I only wanted a cuddle! I were upset, constibble. I barely got out o' that there pub alive. Ay, love – I' ave suffered.'

'Is this your vehicle, sir?' the policeman enquired with a sigh and a practised look of exasperation. 'I'll speak to you in a moment, madam. Could you take your hand out of this gentleman's lap?'

'No, it's MOD,' said Whyte curtly, looking daggers at his sulking passenger. 'I'm a flight sergeant at RAF Winderby.'

'I see. Have you been drinking, sir?' asked the constable.

'I had one pint, that's all,' confirmed Whyte. 'And I didn't have anything to do with what's gone on in there.'

Violet smirked triumphantly. 'I'm afraid I'm the only witness to that, officer,' she said patting the flight sergeant's leg.

'I'm afraid I'm going to have to ask you to take a breathalyser test, sir,' explained the policeman.

'You can do what you want as long as you get her out of my Land Rover – before she pounces on me again.'

'YOU CHEEKY BASTARD! I'LL SHOW YOU "POUNCE"!' she yelled before she threw herself at her rescuer and began to beat him with her fists.

PC Justin Deighton let her have a few more seconds' grace, then pulled her off her cowering paramour before she could do the flight sergeant any harm with her false nails and war bangles. Then the PC made Violet stand outside the Land Rover whilst he breathalysed her resentful date.

★

Back in the Saltersgate Inn, the pub's surviving visitors were enjoying a very different 'mouth-to-mouth' whilst those wardens and Diddy men who were regaining consciousness were arrested and processed, once the landlord had been revived and questioned and the NYMPA committee members had given the law their own side of the story.

Detective Sergeant Broadhead went straight back to Whitby Hospital, to the same ward as PC Jackson Alger and with the same concussion.

Chapter Four

Riff RAF

For Flight Sergeant Alan Whyte, the notorious former 'lothario' of RAF Brize Norton, a three-year exile to RAF Winderby had certainly not been the living hell his more gregarious and sociable colleagues at Brize Norton had painted it to be. Whyte's reputation as the white-hot ladies' man of England's biggest RAF base was something of a puzzle to his present companions, who thus far had seen not a trace of his irresistible charisma. His reputation only existed at all because of his remarkable good looks and tall, athletic frame. As for his personality, he was a shy, unassuming man whose need to avoid emotional conflict meant he found it very hard to say no until it was far too late. His life as a happy, single male at a base like Brize Norton lasted almost as long as the front brake pads on an RAF Lightning.

Flight Sergeant Whyte's punishment for failing to resist the forceful advances of his more assertive female professionals had been a year for each unexpected pregnancy that was now marked on Brize Norton's personnel office's annual-leave planner. After six months in North Yorkshire, he had begun to accept his fate and serve his time. He was at least in no danger of being raped or ravished. After nearly two years in the wilderness, he had almost grown to like the splendid isolation. He had never been much of a man for the outdoors, but he had recently bought himself a brand-new Olympus thirty-five-millimetre camera from Ogmundarson Gate Cameras in Whitborough on Sea, an extendable tripod and the biggest Tamron telescopic lens he could afford – and all because of a chance sighting of a very strange creature at dusk on the lower slopes of the opposite hill some three weeks before.

His first sighting had occurred when he happened to be looking through the eyepiece of the recreation room's spotter scope early one evening; panning across the hills just as sun was beginning to set, he spotted a bizarre, four-legged creature sprinting across the landscape with a rapidity and determination that defied the laws of nature. His first impression of the creature was that it was some large hunting dog of unusual pedigree. It was perhaps the Frankenstein offspring of a brown bear and a gigantic Alsatian, though he had had to revise his first impression when it suddenly stopped running and stood upright with a cat in its mouth.

As Whyte had not made any close friends at his new posting and knew no one in the area, he decided not to share the details of his strange sighting. Instead, he resolved to obtain some photographic evidence, and then present the pictures to a naturalist and the experts at Charlwood Zoo. The thought of being able to have a meaningful conversation with someone off the base had given him a lift and some motivation. It would certainly be a lot safer than going into a pub or a bar on his own without a wingman.

Chapter Five

That Old Devil Called Love

There are four distinct branches of magic.

The first is practised by old, temperamental and learned men, who have beards that sprinkle fossilised crumbs wherever they are sitting.

The second branch is populated by wild-haired women who eschew bras, accumulate cats, and run for years on gin, muesli and cottage cheese, with barely an ulcer.

The third is populated by the young and inexperienced of the first and second branches, who have yet to acquire a mentor, or a following mature and candid enough to tell them that what they think they know about magic is absolute nonsense.

The last and most dangerous branch of the craft is practised by children. For it is only children who are able to conjure up the worst possible combination of words at exactly the wrong moment in time during serious adult conversations. They can also recall exactly where the adults left the funny-shaped plastic turnkey for the gas-meter cupboard door – even when their elders have absolutely no idea at all where it might be.

Within these four branches, there are three lifelines.

One bestows happiness, contentment and a relaxed approach to personal hygiene.

The second corrodes the soul, poisons the mind and keeps the exorcists of the Church of Rome from getting a good night's sleep.

The third leaves terrible stains on tablecloths and aprons.

All the best occultists are distinctly childlike. Only a very few make competent herbalists.

You can never have too many good glass jars.

Chest freezers are great.

Don't store reactive substances in the house.

There are many, many more good pieces of advice for those about to embark on their own path to enlightenment, but it is often the fate of the young that they prefer to speak but do not listen – thus accidentally becoming fodder for the boiler of natural selection, rather than surviving to maturity. As the members of the four branches move towards their middle years, self-destruction, true knowledge or a more effective brand of stain remover, they acquire the adjectives and pronouns appointed to them by their peers and those behind them on their path to their place in history. There are enough of these titles in magical tradition to satisfy even the most entitled and pedantic of occultists. The most coveted are bestowed by the Atlantean, Egyptian or Greek masters operating in the higher planes of the astral kingdom. A title awarded in Latin is less so, though Latin spoken well – by anyone in a good cloak – never fails to impress the ignorant.

Ritual conducted in Latin sounds impressive to the layman and is sometimes almost musical in its pronunciation. Every letter, vowel and consonant is pronounced in its hard form. As long as the adept knows his or her script, follows all the guidance and disinfects their circle, there is little room for error. Though there is also little room to make a name for oneself.

Unfortunately, the most lasting reputations are made on the edge of catastrophe, where the most mercurial and curious talents gravitate. The recipes of Atlantean, Egyptian and the more radical strands of contemporary ritual are often exciting, but they are also worryingly incomplete. Only the most competent of the brave can go to the edge of disaster and return unharmed, though their hair often turns a frightening shade of white – some occultists think this makes them look rather buff.

Although the various occult societies and groups do not have their own systems of honours, they have distinct hierarchies of competence. Generally speaking, the better the witch or wizard, the harder they are to find. The very best may even have their own castellated mansion – and if they are doubly blessed, it may even be on a private plot on an offshore island, surrounded by a great big, mossy wall.

Whitborough had one such lady, a sorceress for whom the title 'occult trouble shooter' was absolutely appropriate. She was presently engaged in performing a banishing ritual for a former close personal friend – Derek Beautimann, the grand wizard of the accident-prone Black Hand Coven – who had a stubborn though much reduced demon to offload before he could get all of his clothes back, though his host wasn't in any great hurry to reunite him with his boxer shorts. Their ritual was now in full swing and was attracting exactly the kind of company that would make most sane people's hair fall out. Even before it had had the chance to turn a 'buff' shade of white.

In the great Martello tower of Derek's host, all hell

was breaking loose(in the truest sense of the word), as the first demonic outriders and escorts of the demon Tetarzepamdomestoz – Hell's minister for mines, caves and underground car parks – arrived from the underworld to take home the much humiliated and diminished seed of their master. Tetarzepamdomestoz normally manifested at full strength as a luminous hot-air-balloon-sized globe of rancid saliva, pus and snake venom – in his proper proportions. However, since his second unfortunate encounter with the gun-slinging witches of the Black Hand Coven, he was now reduced to the size of a TicTac and was trapped inside the orb of a lead-glass marble, thanks to Violet Penrose's talisman, and several jets of gin and holy water from Joy Blanchard's atomiser. The indignity of his prison was almost too much for him to bear. His numerous minions were also far from pleased, stalking the circle of protection uselessly for a weak point, whilst trying not to attract the attention of the woman in the centre, who was dispatching their braver compatriots with a ruthlessness that they might have admired had she not been mortal and Russian.

Glowing, red coals wearing cackling demonic faces flew dizzy loops around the two occultists' protective circle, belching grey smoke and sparks like a demonic tribute to the Red Arrows, whilst the demon's attendant swarm of emerald-green blowflies flew anticlockwise to the orbs in an insane game of chicken.

New forms of cadaverous ghouls materialised and began to circle, jostling and pushing against the protective ring of salt and chalk inscriptions. The excitement of seeing so many of Hell's fiends on an empty stomach was all too much for Derek, who was keeping his good eye firmly shut. Sveta, engrossed in her scrolls, seemed to be taking no notice at all of the furious, misshapen ghouls stalking the edge of the circle, until a particularly tall and aggressive example tried overturn a scrying bowl near the hearth.

It had barely begun its intentional act of mischief before it disappeared in a cloud of steam, dispatched with handful of rock-salt crystals and sloe berries, then a half-empty gin bottle shattered against the fireplace, vaporising another half dozen of its friends. Sveta Anchbadze, the Annie Oakley of Occultism, was just getting started...

The black glass marble in the iron dish resting on top of Derek's solar plexus now began to make some serious heat as the demon's companions returned from the pits of Hell to reclaim their much slighted colleague. As the marble spread it's warmth though the thin, iron saucer to Derek's naked chest, getting hotter with every passing second, Sveta slipped a thick, padded deerskin pouch underneath it, and spat out a mouthful of juniper berries and gin into the saucer – to stop their demon prisoner from getting above himself – whilst she re-read the next verse of her invocation and stared down the army of fiends. Tossing random handfuls of rock salt at the boldest and angriest to put them firmly in their place.

'You're enjoying this, aren't you?' hissed Derek, flinching from the falling sparks and hot, acrid smoke trails choking the perimeter walls of the tower.

'Not at all I am not, but is nice to see such fine, manly legs and a manly chest again,' replied Sveta pushing her naked leg out of the waist-length slash in her skin-tight velvet dress. 'You like bodice?' she asked.

'Very nice,' said Derek without much sincerity, just as another fiend attempted to break into their circle. Sveta stamped her foot and tossed another grenade of rock salt into its aura for the crime of drawing Derek's attention away from her ankle. It disappeared in a cloud of sparks and smoke, taking out three more of its terrified companions and leaving a foul aftertaste of sulphur. The black marble – now sufficiently hot – had started to melt, and a much reduced Tetarzepamdomestoz began to coalesce over the triangle of art, looking as small and glum as any significant demon stuck with the beak of a herring gull as it's only means of communication.

Sveta brought up a silver-capped hazel branch in her left hand and a banishing pentacle boss in her right to let her adversary know exactly what kind of lady it was dealing with before she began her speech. 'I order thee, Tetarzepamdomestoz, to return from whence thou came and let no malice or injury exist between us. Return now with all thy company now here and remain in thy kingdom until such time as I choose to summon thee, if it pleases me. Go now and heed my words, for I am woman, sorceress and mother of the book, and thou wilt obey me, in the name of Cernunnos and Aradia. Go now and peace be upon thee.'

Suddenly, all the fiends around their circle vanished in a sudden gust of wind, and the candles in their storm lanterns guttered violently before flaring up and settling back into a lackadaisical shimmy. A strange quiet filled the void.

Derek watched the snot-green puddle in the iron dish drain away from one dimension to the next and wondered when his host was likely to offer him his clothes back. Sveta tossed a handful of rock salt into the inner space of the triangle of art once their demon prisoner had completely disappeared, and then lit four incense sticks, placing them at the north, south, east and west stations of their protective inner circle. Next, she bound a sheaf of hazel twigs, which she proceeded pass through each column of smoke as a precursor to her final banishing ritual. It had all been a bit too much for Derek, who was already feeling rather queasy after his meal of lobster and seaweed. Presently, he fainted.

Chapter Six

The Luckless Banshee of Dickie Hapeknee's Lane

A stray thermatick magic bolt from Sveta Anchabadze's hazel wand had inadvertently reincarnated the lost remains of Whitborough's most famous witch, Mrs Mothersole, who had now returned to stalk the rich verges of Dickie Hapeknee's Lane, which was the place where she had spent so many happy evenings excavating mandrakes and collecting herbs when she was still mortal and breathing.

Mrs Mothersole's first few hours as a reincarnated banshee had proved rather frustrating. The narrow lane and it's avenue of trees that had protected and concealed her in life was now a very different place. The protective avenue of trees and the gently winding earthen path within had gone, and had been replaced by a brutal strip of compacted gravel and tar marked by strange painted lines, overlooked by tall, wooden posts carrying thin, black cords. She had wailed and shrieked and squelched at several cars and minicabs that had passed along its length only to be jeered and yelled at by their occupants, who thought they were being pranked by students from the nearby sixth-form college, because it was Rag Week.

Despite a number of false starts, and a near miss with a speeding milk float, the dead witch's miserable spectre had persevered with her lot, perfecting her posture and vocal projection as she trudged pitifully up and down the long, undulating road between Seamer village and Sandybed Top until just before dawn, when she heard the distant rumble of a large lorry accelerating towards her puddle at the bottom of one of the many rolling depressions along the lane.

Her new look, which could be best summed up as a saturated Sarah Brightman modelling a seaweed empire dress, was destined to be a very short incarnation. When she was alive, Mrs Mothersole had been kindly, warm and mischievous. Undead and dripping wet, she could do very little but squelch, screech and gurgle.

As her nemesis, the first MacKenzie Dye builders' merchant's delivery lorry of the morning bore down on her puddle, she tried one last time to get her wailing right.

'EEEEEEEEEEE!' cried the waterlogged banshee, raising two blotchy, white arms above her wet head as the lorry's blinding headlights peeped over the crest of the rise above her.

'GRROOOOAAAAAARRRRRRRR!' replied the seven-and-a-half-tonne flatbed truck, with six tonnes of hardcore vibrating in tune with the six-litre diesel engine as it reached the crest of Dickie Hapeknee's Lane's third hump and thundered down the other side.

As it was only 5.30am and the road was still empty, the driver – Tommy Todd – took his eyes off the road and tried to tune into Radio Whitborough, oblivious to the banshee in her tatty, black shroud who had raised her voice several octaves and was only moments away from being flattened by a mud-spattered registration plate with thirteen and a half tonnes of speeding steel and hardcore behind it.

'EEEEEEEEEEEK!' screamed the banshee again as the

truck reached fifty-five miles per hour at the bottom of the dip in the road, just before her puddle, then the DAF lorry struck the saturated corpse girl with a brutal smack and crushed her as flat as a moth between two paving slabs. The truck's huge leaf-spring suspension did not even flex as the huge tyres on the rear double axel turned what was left of Mrs Mothersole into a squelchy soup of seawater-saturated gore before the truck roared on towards the next hillock to the blare of Gloria Gaynor's 'I Will Survive' and Tommy Todd's post-cigarette phlegm clearout.

A tubby hedgehog, the only witness to Mrs Mothersole's disastrous stand-off, heard a self-pitying whimper and a burp from the puddle, then ambled off dejectedly in search of more slugs.

Chapter Seven

Ironsides Rides Again

Inspector Marshall's return to duty at Whitborough Police Station was somewhat hampered by his new NHS-issue wheelchair's refusal to navigate around furniture and architecture that had never been designed for wheelchairs. He did at least have the use of a lift.

Eventually, his superior – Superintendent D'Ascoyne – had to admit defeat and consent to Inspector Marshall's request to provide a temporary servant from their admin pool once his desk had been raised high enough for him to get his knees underneath. But, once he had learned that his esteemed colleague had been hospitalised with a suspected skull fracture, he began to have second thoughts about his return to duty.

Inspector Marshall was beginning to feel distinctly uncomfortable inside Whitborough Police Station. He decided to call his on his colleague George Broadhead as soon as he could think of a pretence to get away from his desk, and he had a growing feeling that he was being set up as the stationary duck on someone else's rifle range.

Chapter Eight

Burning Love

As one demon returned to hell from Landkey Island, with its beak between its legs, the supernatural guardians of the infamous Treasure of the Mar del Norte – Tapas-Molinos,-for Spain, and his partner in Hell, the Mayan demon Quetzlcarbon Yum Taxx – began to make their next contributions to the misery and mayhem they had already begun during the Easter bank holiday weekend.

Thwarted by the sixth sense of the equally dangerous Caledonian Mafiosi Barnett Crosbie, who had fled the town with a third of the Drake brothers' gold, the two murderous entities re-focussed their destructive energies on the two static portions of the treasure that were still in the borough. The curse of the treasure could only harm its English-born vendors, and the Scottish fugitives were immune to its effects, forcing the two demonic entities to concentrate their energies in Whitborough. Tapas-Molinos now attacked the cache in the Adidas tote bag locked in Derek Beautimann's filing cabinet, whilst Yum Taxx went to work on the portion left in the Snap-on tool chest resting in Brian Drake's garden shed.

Brian's shed was damp, dusty and cold, and there was nothing even remotely combustible inside that Yum Taxx could work with. So far, heating the gold to a cautious 500 degrees Celsius (under half its melting temperature) had only managed to melt the four plastic sacks of chicken-mature compost that were stacked around the toolbox and create the most unholy stink on Bader Drive since the sewers dried out in the long, hot summer of 1976.

Tapas-Molinos, by contrast, was having a much better evening. Derek Beautimann's sports bag was now alight, and the flames were beginning to spread to the card, paper and wooden picture frames in the upper drawers, buckling the thin metal of his office filing cabinet. The fire inside now began to draw in even greater amounts of cool, clean air through the buckled seams of the cabinet, which accelerated the conflagration. Soon, the fire began to warp the thin sheet steel at the back of the cabinet, letting its flames char the oak wainscoting on the lower part of the wall behind and popping the strings on Derek's best squash racket.

Derek, oblivious to the fire, was brushing his teeth in the family bathroom before bed. His wife had just passed the study on her way to the airing cupboard on the first-floor landing when she stopped suddenly and sniffed the air.

'Derek?' she asked.

'Yes, what it is?'

'Is Grace making toasted sandwiches again?'

'I don't know. Why?'

'I can smell something burning.'

'I'm just finishing up,' he said from their bathroom. 'I'll be out in a second.'

Passing the study door again, Derek's wife saw smoke coming out from under the bottom of the study door. 'DEREK!'

Chapter Nine

An Evening's Entertainment at the Esteemed
Valhalla Retirement Home

A few streets away from the Beautimann residence, Elsie
Cakebread – the first lady of Whitborough's legendary
Valhalla Retirement Home – had just finished her lunch a
double fish-finger sandwich and was contemplating a healthy
choice tangerine with her Jack Daniels and coke when the
phone rang.

Valhalla catered for the kind of ladies and gentlemen who
had no intention of being passive, polite or bored in their
twilight years, and so it was always full. If you had heard only
half of what was known about Elsie, Mark and Valhalla, you
would be prepared to believe almost anything. You would
certainly want to pause or reduce the pace of your stride, if
you happened to be walking past her gate, just in case there
was something exciting in progress – and nowhere else in
Whitborough were there so many households in such a
small area with so many pairs of binoculars. Elsie and Mark's
residents, who were at least as interesting as their hosts, could
not help but add to the legend with whatever they did and
wherever they went.

The previous autumn, on Halloween, Valhalla's Hammer
Horror theme party had cut off whole streets around their

plot with a fog bank so dense that the visibility in Ramsgill was on a par with the bottom of Loch Ness – all thanks to one of their guests who had used his old contacts to borrow ten event-standard smoke machines that were laying idle for a month before Alice Cooper's winter tour.

On Bonfire Night, they'd had a firework display of black market Alaskan Coastguard distress rockets, which was visible in Bridlington ten miles away and was seen by at least two high-altitude commercial flights between Frankfurt and Glasgow.

They'd had a Viking funeral on Peaholm boating lake, which made the front page of the *Whitborough Evening News*, and a St Patrick's Day leprechaun wrestling tournament on the lawns, which that caused a lunchtime traffic jam the equal of anything in rush-hour London.

It had all added up to another fun-packed season for the residents of Valhalla, and another exciting autumn for the council – who secretly admired Elsie and Mark's chutzpah and cheek, if only for the quality of incidents and the resulting gossip it generated to enliven their day. And that was without mentioning her seances…

⋆

'Bikers and bitches,'

'It's Audrey, Else.'

'Hi hun; what can I do for ya, pet?'

'I just rang to ask if it's all right for me to drop by this afternoon for your thing.'

'You're always welcome here, Aud.'

'Thanks, Else. What's that funny slurping sound?'

'Oh, I'm just licking some ketchup off me fingers; I just made meself a fish-finger sarnie for lunch.'

'Are you still having that sentence thing later?'

'Seance?'

'Aye, that's the one. You don't mind if I sit in then?'

'Have you got someone dead you need to speak to?'

'No, not really. I just fancied some company, y'know.'

'Well, we've got ten in for 6.30pm, pet, so that makes a nice, cosy dozen with me and you. Get yourself round here about 5pm, if you're still up for it. It'll give me time to grab one of our lot if you change your mind.'

'Does it only work if there's twelve then?'

'You've gotta have even numbers, Aud. I don't do odd numbers – it looks better at the table. I don't like being possessed when we're half-cocked. We've got a vicar coming tonight too: the tall, limp one from St Andrews.'

'Him that looks like Charles Hawtrey?'

'That's him. I can't say I've ever had the pleasure before; I've only ever passed him the once – beside the chest freezer in Spar. I can't think why he'd want to come to one o' my circles. We're not even Church of England.'

'Maybe his connection's a bit iffy, Else,' said Audrey sympathetically.

'They do say that priests are the last people that dead folk want to speak to. Prob'ly cos they was the last folk they saw when they was alive. You've never sat with us before, Aud, have you?'

'Well, I didn't want to impose, with us being mates an' all, but I've always been curious to see what goes on at these things o' yours.'

'It'll be lovely to have you, pet. You could do me a favour

55

actually. On your way, would you get me couple o' boxes o' man-sized tissues from Costcutter?' The big ones in the nice printed boxes. Just in case we get ectoplasmic.'

'Ecto…?'

'Plasmic…Ectoplasm, y'know? It's like KY Jelly for dead folks; it helps 'em slide through from the other side.'

'Ugh. Yuk! It doesn't smell does it?'

'Aaah…It's nowt to worry about. Even if you do get a drop on you, it always washes out – well, most of the time. I'll see you later then. Don't forget me tissues!'

'Aye, okay.'

'Come in the kitchen door, round the back. Mark's in the garage this aft', so just nod if he grunts at you on your way past.'

'Is he sitting in too?'

'Nah, he's putting some new brake pads in the Gold Wing and topping up the brake fluid, so we don't end up in the afterlife an' all.'

Chapter Ten

Fire Woman

The blaze started in the Beautimann household by the Spanish guardian spirit of the Treasure of the Mar del Norte, Tapas-Molinos, was now out of control and browning the edges of the opposite site of the door to Derek Beautimann's study. Derek was just about to go in with his soda syphon and a wet bath towel over his head when his wife screamed at him from the top of the staircase.

'DON'T TOUCH THE DOOR HANDLE, DEREK! THE FIRE ENGINE'S COMING!' she yelled.

'WHY DID YOU CALL THE FIRE BRIGADE?'

'WHAT?'

'WHY DID YOU CALL THE FIRE BRIGADE?'

'DEREK, THERE'S A FIRE IN THE STUDY; THE STUDY'S ON FIRE!'

'I CAN DEAL WITH IT MYSELF!'

'Are you all right, Derek?'

'NO! YES!'

'What's the matter?'

'SHITTING BASTARD BOLLOCKS!'

'Derek...*What an earth is the matter with you?* We need to get out before the fire brigade arrives.'

'Where's Grace?'

'I told her to wait by the front gate; what's the matter?'

'I wish I'd never dug it up... I wish I'd never dug that bloody chest up.'

'Chest? What chest? *What are you talking about?*'

'I've had nothing but trouble since we found it.'

'WE?'

'I'VE GOT TO PUT IT BACK!'

'WHAT? WHAT ARE YOU TALKING ABOUT? WHO IS "WE"?'

'THE GOLD IN THE FILING CABINET IN THE STUDY.'

'GOLD?'

'THE TREASURE OF THE MAR DEL NORTE!'

'Can we talk about this outside. We really need to leave – *now*!'

'BUT...'

'*Derek,* if you take another step towards that door handle, I swear to God I will never speak to you again. Please take the towel off your head and put down the soda syphon.'

Chapter Eleven

Turning Japanese

'Afternoon, Mark!'

'Audrey,' responded Mark.

'Is it all right if I go in?' asked Audrey. 'I hope that isn't for you again, ' she added as the wail of fire-engine sirens grew louder.

'Nah. We're not on fire today,' replied Mark running a quick eye over Valhalla's roofline. 'Will you tell 'er indoors I'm nearly done out 'ere? Once I've cleaned up I'm gonna tek the Gold Wing down t'road and test 'er brakes.'

'It's big, isn't it?' Said Audrey admiringly, prodding the king and queen seat of the Cakebreads' Honda Gold Wing. 'I thought they only made cars and pianos, Honda?'

'You're probably thinking of Yamaha, Audrey. They mek bikes and pianos.'

'What's that other one – Nagasaki? They make satsumas, don't they?'

'I think you mean Kawasaki.'

'Blummin' Japanese – they mek everything these days, don't they? When they aren't eating all the bloody whales. I do like your bike though; it looks dead plush.'

'Aye. It's as comfy as any of us chairs, carries us an' all our gear. She'll still do 120 mph even wi' the two of us and all our crap on board.'

'Nice.'

'Can you mek us another tea when you go in, Aud? Me throat's as dry as a bloody sand dune,' said Mark, offering Audrey a mug that looked as though it had been used to bail out the bilge in a canal barge. 'It's all right, Aud; it's just good, honest muck. Just give it a quick rinse under the tap.'

'*Mark, it's disgusting!* How on earth have you been using this to drink from? 'she cried, holding the blackened mug at arm's length between her thumb and forefinger.

'Quick rinse an' it 'll be reet!'

Five minutes of dedicated scrubbing later, the mug was as nearly as clean as the day it was bought and returned full of dark-brown tea to its careless owner, with its grime-free transfer print of Linda Lusardi grinning anew.

'You didn't have to clean it that well, Audrey lass!'

'I had to use neat Fairy Liquid and a pot scrubber on her face, you mucky sod.'

'Eh?'

'Linda Lusardi. You should recognise her – she were on your mug.'

'Oh aye, so she is; thanks, girl!'

'Don't put your grubby fingers on her boobs you mucky beggar.'

Chapter Twelve

I Fought the Law

'So here we are again amongst the cripples,' said a glum Inspector Marshall, as he sat next to the bed of his injured colleague Detective Sergeant Broadhead on the fracture ward in Whitby Hospital.

'It's a shit sandwich this case, guv. We're well out of it,' stated Broadhead.

'Are you gonna spin out your leave, George?' enquired Marshall.

'The doc says it's just concussion.'

'It's bad enough having concussion.'

'I can't sleep properly, I can't read because I can't focus my eyes, an' I feel sick all the bloody time. My head's throbbing, Ray.'

'Are you going to have a dent in your forehead?'

'I bloody hope not. I don't know what I'm gonna find when the pad and the bandages come off.'

'All this bloody trouble has made me give some serious thought to taking early retirement – after a decent interval on long-term sick. I didn't sign on to get blown up and shot at. Just look at the pair of us. My dad was in a better state than the two of us when he got back from the beach at Dunkirk.'

'I'll make up my mind when this lot comes off,' said

Broadhead, patting the side of his head gently. 'If I have to walk around with a bloody great sword-pommel scar on my forehead, I'll be pulling a sickie too. But what else are we gonna *do*?' I don't want to be off the force. It's the only bloody thing I know.'

'My thoughts entirely, George. There's no way in hell some jumped-up clowns from London are forcing us out, but, the way things look, we need to get ourselves on the sick and out of their sight. Only on temporary basis, just until all this shit blows over. I'm not going to carry on as if nothing's happening when there's a distinct possibility that we're being lined up as someone else's fall guys. Sod that for a game of soldiers…'

'I thought I'd be safe in the Saltersgate Inn. Who'd have thought they'd have the biggest scrap since that business in the Bunch of Keys between the Milk Race and the Navy. What kind of bloody nutcase uses a bullet belt on a fella dressed up like a Diddyman? What's wrong with using your fists?'

'Doddy's fan club were using the landlord's swords and spears collection, George. That's what the bikers said.'

'Blimey! They breed them mean in Knotty Ash, don't they?'

'I thought you might have noticed they were tooled up when you steamed in from the bar like the Sweeney.'

'I can't remember anything after draining me second pint, guv. The doctor says memory loss is common with concussion.'

'These things are sent to try us,' muttered Marshall, shifting his weight on his wheelchair cushion from one cheek to the other.

Chapter Thirteen

Carry On Possessing

At 6.30pm, Elsie and Grant drew the curtains in the Gold Cup Lounge and set up her twelve-chair roundtable before Grant ushered in the other guests waiting in the vestibule.

'Evening, everybody. One chair each an' no spreading out!' cackled Elsie as she collected everyone's invitation cards. 'I'll just introduce meself and a couple of our guests, as we've got a few new faces with us tonight. I'm Elsie, I run this wonderful little retirement home called Valhalla with me 'usband Mark; it's me who's channelling the spirits tonight. Anyone not been to a seance before, apart from Audrey… and the vicar? We'll go round the table now – deosil – an' you can all introduce yourselves one at a time, like.'

'Deosil?' asked Audrey with a puzzled frown.

'Clockwise, Aud. As everyone knows me, thee an' the rev, we can start with you two,' said Elsie, revealing two ranks of carnivorous teeth behind her pursed lips. 'What're your names?' she asked of the formally attired couple in the four and five o'clock positions at their table.

'We're from the Psychic Society, Mrs Cakebread,' said the gentleman. 'I'm Nicolas and this is Janet,' he said, turning towards his colleague.

'The *Psychic Society*, eh?' replied Elsie. 'Checking up on me, are yer?'

'I wouldn't put it quite like that, Mrs Cakebread,' said Janet calmly.

'Well, since it's too late to start buggering about vetting you all, you can stay put; just so long as you sit still an' behave yourselves. But you're not gonna see any funny goings on in this house.'

'That's very nice to hear, Mrs Cakebread,' added the lady.

'Else.'

'Elsie,' said Janet obligingly.

'No, it's Else, Jan.'

'Of course,' said Janet, trying to conceal a sudden instinct to run.

'I would like to point out that I've attended several exorcisms, Mrs Cakebread,' interjected the vicar.

'All right, vicar; we'll get round to you in a minute. We ain't chucking any holy water around in 'ere tonight by the way. Before you all start getting worried, no one' ere's in danger of getting possessed by demons. I won't 'ave 'em in the 'ouse.'

'That's very reassuring of you to say so, Mrs Cakebread. But one can't keep the delinquents of the astral planes at bay by sheer force of personality. I don't mean any disrespect, but one needs to take proper precautions,' stated her next guest in line, Diane Dodson from the Whitborough Society of Inner Light, somewhat emphatically.

'It might 'elp speed things up an' keep us all civil if you'd keep your trap shut until it's your turn to speak, pet,' snapped Elsie, putting Mrs Dodson firmly in her place.

'I beg your pardon!'

'My 'ouse, my rules. You don't get to speak until I speak

to you, right? Or you can naff orf. House rules. It were on yer invitation cards, so sit still an' sit tight. Right! Seeing as you're next in line at the six o' clock position, you can say your piece. What's yer name?'

'Mrs Dodson.'

'From?'

'The Society of Inner Light. We follow—'

'Yes, I know who *you* follow. Did you notice the protective layers when you came over our threshold? Or the cord of protection on the floor?'

'Oh, I didn't see it.'

'And what about the rock-salt path around the 'ouse and the crystals in the corners of the room?'

'I'm sorry, I missed those too.'

'Any other advice?'

'No. No. That's very reassuring, Elsie. Else…'

'Quite happy now, are you?'

'Yes. Yes, absolutely.'

'All right with you if I get started, is it?'

'Of course, I didn't mea—'

'Just to reassure the rest of you folk, we've got nearly as many deterrents to demons round 'ere as the bleedin' Vatican. So, don't fret. We're all gonna be sitting still, nicely inside the circle of protection. That's the white cord on the floor we'll join up in a minute.' Said Elsie, looking daggers at Mrs Dodson. 'Once we link hands we don't let go till I say so right? Everyone stays on their chair. No chit-chat or whispering, an' just yes an' no answers. Any messing about and you've got my husband to answer to after our Grant's finished with yer,' Elsie explained, nodding to her left at a huge man in a great big, leather armchair.

'You all know the vicar from St Andrews, Reverend Blueit. Audrey works in the Kenwith Valley Museum as an archivist, and that's Grant over there,' added Elsie, raising a thumb to her enormous doorman. 'Grant takes care of business whilst I'm incapacitated, don't you pet?'

'Yes, Else.'

'You couldn't find a finer lad in North Yorkshire for taking care o' business. Now, a few other rules. No farting, coughing or sneezing whilst I'm possessing. It proper takes it out of you, being full of dead folk. Especially if we get shocked out of coincidence all of a sudden, just cos somebody's sneezed. The eadaches I get from stuff like that is like 'aving three full grown 'angovers the morning after – so no moving an' shouting, or it's an extra twenty quid each to make up for me being flat on me back tomorrow morning.'

'And what do they call you, love?' asked Audrey, locking eyes with Derek Beautimann, but ignoring his plump deputy, Maureen, who was doing her best not to catch Audrey's gaze.

'Derek Mrs Cakebread. It's my first time here.'

'First time here,' parroted Elsie, 'And an educated man too, lovely…Who's your friend?'

'Maureen,' replied Derek, blushing slightly. 'It's her first time too.'

'First time too? And does Maureen speak?' she enquired, looking directly at Maureen.'

'She's a little shy,' said Derek, putting his right shoe over Maureen's toes.

'Shy? Oh bless,' said Elsie. 'She's not so little though, are you love?'

Maureen flushed and gritted her teeth, bashing Derek's knee under the table cloth with her free hand.

'Well, we'd best get started then,' said Elsie, 'By the way, just so's you all know, I've got a nose like a starving shark, so don't think I won't know if any of you lot let a sneaky one out. 'Aving a throat full of someone else's ectoplasm is bad enough, so you can keep your backsides corked till you get outside. And that includes you, vicar.'

'I can assure you, Mrs Cakebread, I'll be doing no such thing.'

Elsie's guests from the Psychic Society and the Whitborough Society of Inner Light were looking as though they were having second thoughts about staying for the duration, but they were too worried about what their host might say if they asked to leave. They sat in silence and tried to keep their misgivings to themselves.

'Anyone need the loo before we start?'

'I think we might just... before we, erm...' mumbled Mr and Mrs Mundy Elsie's gardener and bookkeeper, respectively.

'First floor, end of the corridor, love – and put the seat back down on yer way out. If anyone feels sick, you've all got a waste-paper bin on your left side. Nobody moves until we're done, right? If anyone's got an itchy nose you'll have to rub it on your shirt collar. It's ten quid apiece upfront. Audrey here'll tek yer money before we start.'

'Be a love and switch the lights off, Grant. Draw the curtains first though, will you, pet – whilst I light the candle? There's a good lad.'

Elsie and Grant busied themselves attending to the last few details, then Grant lumbered back to his leather armchair and sat back down with a satisfying crump.

'Everyone comfy? Now I want you lot to link hands, clear your thoughts and—'

Suddenly, there was an urgent knock on the door to the passage.

'Who's that?' yelled their host.

'It's TV licensing, Else. They want to come in and look around…'said Gareth, Valhalla's stargazer, whose favourite pastime was using the telescope in the attic planetarium to spy on passers-by, tourists and drunks staggering up Ramsgill high street.

'Tell 'em to piss off!'

'But—'

'I'm having a circle. Get Mark to deal with 'em,'

'You do have a television licence, don't you, Mrs Cakebread?' asked the vicar politely.

'No.'

'Oh?'

'We ain't got a TV, vicar. You wouldn't buy a driving licence for a dog, would you?'

'No TV at all?' replied the vicar, still trying his best to deconstruct Elsie's last statement. He wasn't at all sure that it wasn't meant to put him off balance.

'No, we ain't.'

'Oh.'

'We've got a cinema room. I don't like TV aerials. They play havoc with me channelling, I get an awful fuzz if I'm anywhere near an aerial when I'm possessing.'

'How extraordinary. I had no idea that television could do that…'

'Well, you ain't psychic, are you, vicar? You're an undertaker and a social worker. You're not jumping in and out of the astral twice a week. Close yer eyes. I can feel Roll-up in me waters. Whatever else you all do, don't break hands.'

'Roll-up?'

'Roll-up, me spirit guide. Used to be a one o' the workshop team at Kawasaki Scarborough before he passed over.'

'*A motorcycle mechanic is your spirit guide?*'

You got a problem with motorcycle mechanics?'

'I, er…'

'He is *dead*, by the way – maybe I didn't emphasise that enough – and not freshly dead either. Knows 'is onions, does Roll-up. He's the best spirit guide I've ever had. I've tried 'em all over the years: Celts, Inuit, Vikings, Incas, Indians, Red Indians – even a bleeding Atlantean Priest. Couldn't understand a bloody word they were saying most of 'em. An' that Atlantean – he were friggin' hopeless if it ever looked like rain.

'Roll-up's been a breath o' fresh air. He speaks proper an' tells it like it is. We had a bit of history before he passed; in fact, it were our Gold Wing that fell on him an' killed him, cos he were more interested in rolling his next fag than checking the safety bolt were reet through the legs on the bike lift. You thinking of going somewhere, vicar?'

'I just realised I left the vestry unlocked, Mrs Cakebread. I…'

Big Grant stood up and walked around their table, then crossed his arms over the head of the guest opposite the vicar.

'You're not leaving now, vicar; we've linked hands…' declared Elsie.

'I'm afraid I must. I—'

'Can't be having a seance with an uneven number. You go an' we've only got eleven. Can't be having an uneven number – it's unlucky. You'll have to stay. *So sit your arse down*,' said Elsie in the sweetest but firmest of voices.

'Right everybody, quiet now – hold hands tight and breathe out slow…Is there anybody there?'

Chapter Fourteen

On the Mend

Albert Gall, North Yorkshire's newest werewolf, was enjoying his liberty and health in the Endeavour bar in Whitby. After two nights in Whitby Hospital, he was now infused with a strange new vigour and warmed by £2,000 in used notes from the man who had liberated his bungalow of its roof.

Albert had also received his initial batch of claims forms from his buildings-and-contents insurance company, and a first emergency payment of £400 to pay for temporary accommodation whilst he arranged the repairs to his home. He had just put down the *Whitby Gazette* at the rooms to let page when his friend Dave the landlord came down to ask him about his health.

'I see you've been in the wars again, Albert. Cracking pair of black eyes you've got there, old fella.'

'Huh! It's me ribs that need the sympathy. Them up at t'hospital thought I'd brokken all of 'em an' ruptured me spleen. It turns out I'm not too bad after all. In fact, I ain't felt so well since I were twenny.'

'Well, that's got to be a good enough reason for a few drinks, hasn't it?'

'That's what I said to t'doc just afore he discharged me. I said two nights in t'hospital was the longest time I've been without a drink. I got fed up with all them poncy consultants telling me that they couldn't understand why I weren't dead. "Nice to see you alive too," I sez to the last one. Cheeky bastards!'

'How's your bungalow, Albert?'

'Well, she's all walls mostly, since me roof got blown off; thanks for asking.'

'So can they save it?'

'Who, the Church?'

'No, your builders, you daft beggar.'

'Ha! Des Mountain and his lads are sorting it. It needs new ribs, joists an' tiles, new ceilings an' a rewire.'

'Pretty big job then?'

'Aye. I'm not sure I won't be on the move again before they've done. Life with me sister ain't exactly happy families,' he moaned. 'She'll kill me with chit-chat, an' tea an' cake if I don't get me sen out soon.'

'Your walls are good then, Albert?'

'Three feet thick my walls. Not much chance o 'them getting blown down. Anyways, the big grass bank between me 'ouse and the gas tank took most of the blast. Its only me roof sits proud of it.'

'There's a three-room bedsit going at the Saltersgate Inn, in the guest cottage, nice and quiet. It's only for five weeks. If you fancy it?'

'Saltersgate, eh? I should be safe from that bow-legged bastard from Devon up there.'

'Who?'

'The twat that scalped me 'ouse.'

'That Kingcombe fella?'

'Aye, that's 'im. Though he did leave me two grand by way

of an apology. An' a get-well-soon card. Jackson and Conn are burying what's left of me Land Rover and smoothing things over with Old Coote – so I'm only out o' pocket on the Landy. Can't claim that one on me insurance unfortunately.'

'How come?'

'I was pissed as a fart when I crashed her.'

Chapter Fifteen

Clash City Records

Brian Drake's clamshell slipper was the funniest thing his customers had ever seen in his shop, apart from the wonderfully kitsch Ozzy Osbourne album sleeves that the Drake brothers had sold so many of. Unfortunately for Brian, a slipper for pensioners with gigantic Velcro lined 'ears' was the only thing he could get to cover up the great bandage on his foot, which he'd had since impaling it on a cavalry sabre. So far, he had managed to keep it out of view behind the counter for most of the day. Embarrassing footwear, however, was the very least of his problems.

If Whitborough police or the two MI5 officers investigating the recent shootings and bombings in the town found out it was him and his staff who were responsible for the biggest mainland terrorist attack in history, he was not going to be at risk of over-exercising himself or his feet for a very, very long time.

To add to his self-inflicted sense of misery, the very thing he had risked life, liberty and peace of mind for was resting under a Shire horse's raincoat in a cabin at Charlwood Zoo. This was the sleeping quarters of a hormonal African black rhino called Edith with irritable bowel syndrome (IBS), terrible gas and a murderous temper.

His other sideline – the slightly less harmful but still illegal purchase and supply of anabolic steroids and growth hormones to the doormen of Whitborough – was not going so well either. Half of his last shipment had been lost or damaged in the surf at Cayton Bay, when his gang's boat had capsized on a reef within sight of the beach.

To avoid refunding his customers, Brian had hatched a plan with his partner to pass off the lost vials with an identical looking fluid that had no beneficial effect on muscle building but made wonderfully fragrant cakes and shortbread. Hypodermic needles that had never seen a mixing bowl of cake mix now dispensed 100cc's of Dorothy Murgatroyd's best concentrated vanilla cake essence into the spotty buttocks of the most intimidating men of the borough with no hope whatsoever of making their hairy backsides light, fluffy or fragrant. Though it would give five of them a very nasty septic cyst and no chance of sitting down for the duration of a week's worth of antibiotics.

★

Brian's brother and business partner, Dave, a vocal critic of his brother's drug dealing, was sitting away from his sibling, outside the shop in the fresh air on the steps of the war memorial, with Michael – their 'Victorian' assistant manager – staring down the twin barrels of his Triton's exhaust pipes.

'Just the bike for Vincent Price, that thing.'

'Thanks Dave. She's a beaut, isn't she?'

'Bloody death trap, more like. Why don't you get a car like Dean's, so you can take Fenella out?'

'I'm afraid my taste in clothes means I can't afford such a fine motor bicycle and a hearse. *And* the insurance…'

'A hearse. *What do you want a bloody hearse for?*' cried Dave, before his thought processes caught up with his mouth. 'On the other hand, it would have to be a hearse for you wouldn't it? I don't think Dean's got any insurance. He booby traps it every time he parks it and sticks that locking spike in the middle of the driver's seat so nobody can nick it.'

'I don't like cars anyway. I like these.'

'You could have both.'

'Not unless I come into some money.'

'Funny you should say that. You can drive can't you?'

'Yeah…Why?'

'How d'you fancy doing a little night errand with Dean – for me and Brian?'

'No, thanks. I can't swim and I don't like jail.'

'Would I ever put your freedom at risk for money, Michael?'

'Brian would.'

'Brian's got bigger problems than us.'

'Yeah. And they're all self-inflicted. Why don't you ask Amie? She used to be a dog handler in the South African police.'

'We're not going to ask Amie exactly because she used to be in the South African police.'

'And I'm a mug?'

'No. You're our last chance to get our gold back, before somebody at the zoo finds it.'

'Gold? What gold?'

'Interested now are you?'

'Are you kidding?'

'No, I'm definitely not kidding.'

'Is this stolen? You've nicked it haven't you?'

'Mmm, not strictly speaking.'

'*What?*'

'Me and misery guts in there,' said Dave, nodding towards Brian in their shop, 'were going after some of the gear Robert left in Cayton Bay. We just happened to see two middle-aged twerps digging a hole on the plateau above the beach. They dug up this big, old strongbox, took half of the stuff inside it, covered their hole in and dumped the rest in a bag in the undergrowth. So when they'd disappeared, we went over to find out what they left behind in the bushes. It was a tote bag of gold coins! These two oldies weren't archaeologists, just ordinary punters. It's not as if this stuff they dug up belonged to 'em. They just got lucky. They were treasure hunters, Mike. They must have had a map of some sort though, cos they knew exactly where to start digging.'

'Do they know you took the bag they left behind?'

'I've no idea. I don't know 'em from Adam.'

'Well, if those two haven't let the museum know yet, you're in the clear.'

'Yeah, that's what we think too. We reckoned they were dodgy, so if we took what they left behind, they wouldn't be able to tell anyone. The perfect crime, you might say…'

'Where's this gold now?'

'Well, half of its under the rubble pile of Mystery City. The other half's in a toolbox under a pile of straw in the rhino enclosure at Charlwood Zoo – thanks to our clueless nephew, who only stuck it there to wind Brian up after Brian asked him to get it out of or garage and hide it somewhere no one would expect to find it. I was just hoping you might like to go and fetch it for us. What'd you say?'

'Aren't rhinos dangerous?'

'So you're not saying no then?'

'Why are you asking me though? It's not as if you're short of mates.'

'Yeah, but they're not like you. Nobody I know can sneak up on people like you can. You're actually downright creepy, you are. If anyone can get in there and sneak it out, you can.'

'What if it wakes up when I'm inside its stable?'

'It won't.'

'Why won't it?'

'Because before it goes to bed, you're going to quietly tip over its water drum and refill it with five pints of Owd Bob, for extra insurance.'

'What, without being seen?'

'Yeah, the water butt's on the dark side of the stable. It's as dark as you need when the sun's gone down.'

'But why would it drink five pints of Owd Bob, Dave?'

'Because elephants and rhinos absolutely love beer. And, every night, the staff put the chalk medicine for its IBS in its water. By the time Edith goes beddy-byes on five pints of Owd Bob, she'll sleeping like a beauty,' muttered Dave. 'She ain't gonna wake up after five pints of Bob. So how about tonight? You can leave that thing at home though...'added Dave, pointing at Michael's bike.

'So, how exactly are we getting there, Dave? Dean's car sounds like a Spitfire and mine's only got one seat.'

'I asked Amie if you can borrow her Mini tonight whilst she's polishing her leg. You two are going in our ninja gear: black balaclavas, gloves and jumpers.'

'Are you sure this is going to work?'

'I have every faith in your ability to sneak in and out without so much as a broken fingernail. Ask Brian to send Deano out from his pit downstairs, will you?'

Chapter Sixteen

The Rhino Burglars

Dean and Michael pulled up at the entrance to Charlwood Zoo after dark in their borrowed Mini 1275GT, and took a slow right turn down the unlit forester's track opposite that led to the old sawmill. It would have been the last-choice route for anyone driving a Mini in daylight, but the darkness concealed it's obvious dangers and less-than-perfect surface. Sure enough, within a very short space of time, Dean had used up nearly all his luck attacking a steep slope strewn with composting chippings that concealed a chaotic cross-hatch of muddy ruts. The Mini's temperature gauge began to creep upwards, towards the red zone.

'Dean…!'

'I know, I know…Hold onto somethin'. It's flatter over the other side where the clearing is,'

'SLOW DOWN!'

'I've been up here before in the Mexico, so chill out,' said Dean, referring to his rally-spec Ford Escort.

'But not in Amie's bloody Mini!' cried Michael, just as the end of a log caught the tiny car's front bumper. The tiny car shuddered and hesitated for a few seconds, as if it were shrugging off a sudden concussion, then they began to slide backwards on the slippery carpet of rotting bark. There was

a horrible, metallic, wrenching noise and several loud pops as the bumper's rivets parted company with the car's front sill.

'*Oh terrific!* Now the bumper's come off… and we're sliding backwards – again!'

'I'm just trying to find some bloody grip on the chippings,' snapped Dean, changing up a gear and backing off the revs to gain traction.

'*Please don't crash the Mini!*' pleaded Michael as his co-conspirator finally managed to find some grip and pushed the car's nose over the crest of the hillock to safety, as the front tyres span like Ferris wheels, spraying the air behind them with rotting chippings.

Finally, the two record-store assistant commandos breathed a sigh of relief as the Mini settled on something approaching flat ground, and they stopped to survey their new vantage point. Behind the car's headlights, the world was as black and impenetrable as the night sky. Dean turned off the engine and popped the bonnet hatch to help the exhausted car cool down.

'That were exciting, weren't it?'

'You're a loon, Beadle… Amie's going to kill you.'

'I'll buy her some flowers…'

'You've torn her bloody bumper off.'

'Okay, then; maybe not.'

'Are you planning to leave her Mini in the middle of this?'

'Course not. We're gonna leave it over there,' he said nodding at some unseen place in the blackness outside.

'Where's there?' asked Michael curiously.

'There's a bit of flat clearing on the right side of us,' said Dean tapping his driver's side window with his finger.

'A clearing filled with ruts and potholes?' enquired Michael sarcastically.

'No more ruts on this side, mate. Flat as a snooker table, this bit here.'

After a long interval, during which they examined Brian and Dave Drake's carefully drawn map with Amie's tiny flashlight, Dean started the Mini again and swung it around to the right. Then, without any warning, they hit a freshly gouged rut and rebounded on their springs. Michael cracked his elbow on the door trim and the side of his head on the seatbelt anchor.

'OUCH!'

'You all right, Mike?'

'NO, ACTUALLY, I'M NOT – YOU MANIAC.'

'Aww, thanks, mate.'

'If we get back to Whitborough in one piece, I'm going to kill you.'

'Not if the rhino gets us first,' said Dean, switching off the ignition and unbuckling his seat belt, 'Fancy a slug of the strong stuff before we set off?' He grinned and offered Michael a small, metal flask full of something that smelled like Richard Burton's breath.

'Me, drink that? You must think I'm stupid.'

'It's only calvados and sherry…'

'No, thanks. I'll pass. My liver is actually one of my oldest friends.'

Dean and Michael knew nothing whatsoever about rhinos. Michael had never 'broken in' to anything, and they had certainly never sneaked into a zoo full of dangerous wild animals, but what they did have was years of experience stepping over inebriated friends in dimly lit nightclub corridors, sneaking into concerts without paying, and a talent for creeping back into their respective homes and bedrooms without waking their parents up. They were probably the only people in Brian and Dave Drake's circle of friends who could break into a rhino's enclosure and come out with all their limbs intact. They also had plenty of black clothes and a watering can full of fresh beer to sedate their victim from the Shirestones Hotel in Cloughton.

'So what did Dave promise *you* to get you out here, Mike?' asked Dean taking another mouthful of liquid from his flask.

'A car.'

'A car! AWWWOW!' Dean croaked, gurning as his tipple ran down the back of his throat like alcoholic napalm.

'I told him I wanted a hearse, actually. I see by your expression this was a lot more than he promised you. Or is that look of disgust down to that drain cleaner you've just been drinking?'

'Huh! I'll be having words with Drakey when we get back. 'OOF, THAT'S GOOD!' gasped Dean after another quick swig.

'I told him unless it's a hearse, I'm not interested. What have you really got in that flask, Beadle?'

'Calvados and sherry, I told you. An' a few slugs of whisky.'

'You're certifiable, you are.'

'By the way… if he buys you one – a hearse, that is – are you and Fen are going to take turns lying in the back? The Adams Family does Tesco?'

'What a good idea!'

'You are crazy, Michael.'

'You're the one drinking the alcoholic equivalent of caustic soda. If one is going to be Gothic, it's worth doing well.'

'Fair point. I should be going on a five-star holiday for what I've done for those two this last month. Now I'm breaking into a bleedin' zoo in the dark to nick a bloody toolbox. Mind you, if I'm right about what's in it, we'll all be quids in tomorrow.'

'What would that be?'

'See this?' said Dean, producing an old gold coin from his leather jacket's pocket, 'Dave gave me this; it's worth a packet. That toolbox is full of 'em.'

'For what we are about to receive, may the Lord make us truly thankful.'

'I ain't joking; it's real gold you know – straight up!'

'Is it really?' asked Michael, his eyes fixed on the coin.

Dean put it quickly back into his pocket.

'Yeah, it's pukka old gold; I thought that'd get your attention. You sure you're ready then?'

'No, but if it's full of coins like that, I'll just have to ignore my conscience.'

'Right,' said Dean, pulling down his balaclava, 'since you're assistant manager and you're getting a car outta this, you can carry the beer. I'll carry the toolbox back.'

'We're not going through the main gate, I trust, wearing balaclavas, are we?'

'Not dressed like pyjama-party ninjas, we ain't. We're going to get to the rhino house from the path around the side by the big trees, like was shown on the map. We'll sneak along the wall in the dark and get this ale in its water barrel, then sod off and hide out downwind out of sniffing range until big Bertha's comatose.'

'Is that the same way Brian and Dave got in?'

'Dunno. It's the only plan I've got, buddy. Let's get going.'

'It's called Edith by the way.'

'What is?'

'The rhino.'

Dean and Michael pulled on their gloves, then climbed out of the Mini and opened the rear doors. Dean took out the watering can of beer and gave it to Michael, then put his right arm through the handle of a large, black rucksack and lifted it from the back of their borrowed car.

'Are you set?'

'Let's do it.'

Charlwood Estate's perimeter wall had been built slowly and purposefully in a time when there were no deadlines, plenty of willing labourers and men who took extraordinary pride in building things that could outlast generations of their own descendants. It was Whitborough's equivalent of the Great Wall of China and would certainly have bankrupted the Warner-Woollens dynasty if it had been the only barrier around the whole estate. As it was, the remaining four-fifths of the estate's border was protected by a fast-flowing river, which provided very good fishing for the family's guests from its steep sheltered banks. Built in milled Scottish granite to a minimum height of twelve feet and with reinforcing buttressing, it was almost as imposing as the walls of Whitborough Castle and an unexpected surprise for any newcomers on a woodland walk.

Dean and Michael followed the narrow path strewn with

pine needles that weaved its way between the great trunks of the tall Scots pines ringing the estate, making good time on the easy contours and flat ground in the light of the moon, without having to use their torches. Eventually, they came to a fork in the path signposted for Cloughton village to the south and the Charlwood salmon bridge to the north-west. Dean took off his rucksack, set it on the ground beside the wall, and started to unbuckle the straps on the main carrying compartment.

'What are you hiding in there, Beadle?' asked Michael.

'The knotted rope and the grappling hook I use to get into Glastonbury and Donington mate. There's no festival I can't get into…'Dean grinned.

'You've done this sort of thing before then?'

'Oh aye. Been climbing walls with this rope since I saw *When Eagles Dare* as a nipper.'

'I can't imagine why.'

'You ever fancied yourself as the Milk Tray man, Mike? Instead of a vampire.'

'Fenella doesn't like chocolates, and I don't relish scaling cliffs. And, since she's taken up fencing, it wouldn't be safe for anyone to go crawling through our sash window. She'd have your eyeball for a shish kebab.'

'She's good with that blade, is she?'

'Fatal. Can you smell something acrid around here? I just caught an awful whiff of something coming off that pile of rocks down there,' said Michael, nodding towards the outline of an old lime kiln built into the bank below them.

'It's the country, innit? You're never far away from a pile of shit in the country. Or summat that died. It's probably a dead badger. I'll go first shall I?'

'*Pardon?*'

'Over the wall.'

'*Ah!* Yeah, okay – if you like.'

'What did you think I meant?'

'Sorry. I was thinking of something else. I just felt like someone walked over my grave. How are we getting the watering can full of beer over the wall?'

'I've got a bit of twine for that. I'll lower it down for ya when I'm up on top. Just step back for a sec whilst I swing me hook up. I'd duck, by the way, if I were you…Just before I swing it.'

'I'll go and stand by that rock pile,' said Michael. 'I can cope with bad smells easier than having your grappling hook in my ear.'

'Good idea, mate,' said Dean, as he made ready to swing his steel climbing hook.

A few seconds later, the thick, steel anchor flew over the wall, making a satisfying thunk as it caught in a thick maw of ivy. Dean tested the rope with a few strong tugs then he turned to alert his partner in crime. He was a little puzzled that Michael wasn't paying the slightest attention to his efforts, had switched on his torch, and was peering queasily at the open side of the rock kiln, looking even whiter than usual.

'Mike? Mike, are you all right?'

'No.'

'What you doing?'

'Come over here, quick.'

'Did you find out what that stink is?'

'It's not a *what*. It's a *them*. Or what's left of them.'

Dean walked over to where Michael was standing and

came face to face with a heap of human body parts still dressed in what remained of their catering whites. The pile of heads and limbs was clumsily stacked in a raked-out depression in the ground inside the stone kiln, and carelessly covered with pine branches and leaves. An arm and part of a shoulder – without the neck and head – toppled off the pile as Michael nudged the stack with a branch. It fell with a horrible splat, just in front of their feet, still wrapped in a bloodstained, white polo shirt with the legend 'Crescent Moon Kebabs' embroidered on the chest. There was also a black-and-white chequered yachting shoe of the type favoured by chefs, with a foot still in it; a well-chewed rubber ball attached to a plaited rope; several punctured tennis balls; and a slipper. The boys from Clash City Records had found Lindsay Boldwood's larder.

'HOLY SHIT, MAN…'cried Dean.

'I'm just going over there a minute…' said Michael queasily, I need some air.'

It's a bleedin' serial killer's larder! exclaimed Dean, and then said something so coarse that it cracked the bark on the Scots pines.

After a few minutes of coughing and retching, Michael returned to his partner in crime.

'Are you all right, Mike?'Dean asked.

'Can we just get over that damn wall and get this over with – before whoever stacked this lot that comes back?'

'I'm right behind you, buddy.' Mumbled Dean.

Chapter Seventeen

Smoking in the Boys' Room

'Is there anybody there?' whispered Elsie, leaning into the back of her chair as she fell into a half-trance, her lips expectant.

The single pillar candle on the table began to flicker and flare. Maureen Moment leaned into Derek's shoulder as if she was about to say something, but Audrey cut her off with one of her looks.

'Oh my goodness!' mumbled the vicar, as two swelling trails of dense, white smoke began to uncoil from Elsie's nostrils, accompanied by the overpowering stink of Duckham's Chainguard and oil-stained, paper hand towels.

'*Shush!*' hissed Elsie, kicking the vicar's ankle. 'Is that you, Roll-up?'

There was weak echo of muffled coughing and the faint ding of something metal being dropped onto a concrete workshop floor in a far off realm.

'Roll-up, put them bloody spanners down an' talk to the old girl, you mucky bugger!' A few seconds passed before the next ding and then a sudden draught carrying a stream of obscene curses stirred the hair on Elsie's sitters; it was quickly followed by a long hacking cough and the sound of someone clearing their throat.

'Roll-up, you dirty bastard, I've got guests here you know…'

'Oooh! What's that disgusting smell?' mouthed Audrey to Grant, who shook his head and raised his finger to his lips.

'Will you leave them bloody bikes alone, Roll-up, and tell me who you've got?'

'Elsie Cakebread, the one and only…'said someone dead, tired and grimy.

'Now then, Rolly, how's life on the other side, pet?'

'Nice to see you too,' said the distorted disembodied voice. Another tool fell to earth with a loud clatter. 'Don't g' near the chainguard on me camping gaz stove, boy!'

'You got any trade for me, Roll-up?'

'Trade for you! I'm tripping over dead folk in 'ere, Cakebread. You can speak to the one with 'is 'ead in his lap first, who's sitting on the tyres next to me compressor, he's giving us all the creeps.'

'I've got a few people here with questions, Roll-up.'

'Give us a second will you, Else? I've gotta get this bleedin' exhaust in position.'

The sound of two men panting as they manhandled something hollow and metallic postponed the conversation momentarily.

'Pass us a three-eighths socket an' the extender, lad, come on! Sharpish!' barked Roll-up, to the spirit of the young, one-armed man who was supposed to be minding his astral torque wrench.

'I wish you'd leave them bikes alone when we're talkin', Roll-up,' grumbled Elsie, 'Who's that lad you got there?'

'I can't slow down for no one now, lass. I gotta get this old Kawasaki triple ready for tonight. Special customer.'

'You got an apprentice, Roll-up?'

'Aydin, 'e calls 'imself. Used to work at Crescent Moon Kebabs until Wolfie 'ere took a shine to 'im an' 'is arm. The lad's doing 'is best, but he's not got both 'is arms, see, and two's the minimum for spannering generally. Anyway, I'll pass you over to Dog-breath, first – it's 'is fault the poor kid's in' ere.'

'WHO?'

'The one who's sat on the pile o' tyres 'ere with 'is 'ead on 'is lap. Boldwood, he calls 'imself. Used to be the landlord of the Shirestones Hotel - he got 'is 'ead chopped off by some farmer at Kettleness. He smells like a wet Rottweiler, smells worse than the chainguard…'he muttered checking the softly bubbling cake tin of high-melting-point chain lube.

'I don't wanna speak to no werewolf, Roll-up; I wanna find out what's causing all this trouble in the borough.'

'Well, he's your man – or dog…'

'All right,' puffed Elsie, 'send the dead bugger down for a minute or two, but don't you go disappearing whilst I'm possessin'; we've got a few other questions – haven't you, vicar?'

'Errr…'squeaked the vicar.

Nicolas and Janet from the Psychic Society looked as if they had made up their minds to run, until they realised that big Grant, Elsie's 'doorman', had been watching their game of footsie and was now scowling at them in a most unfriendly way. They decided to remain seated and take their chances.

Suddenly, a horrible growl burst from Elsie's throat, the candle on the table went out in a rush of wind and the cloud of white mist pouring from Elsie Cakebread's nostrils grew brighter, fortified by an umbilical cord of glowing, white plasma from her mouth. The lycanthrope landlord of Cloughton village was manifesting to speak through the lady of Valhalla. It was not the kind of conversation that most of her guests were expecting to hear, a stream of orders that read like a telegram with barely a hello or goodbye…

'Tell my nephew to make sure he cleans the beer lines every week, tell him to check the brewery's inventory before he signs the delivery note, tell him to stop dressing like a yobbo, tell him to take what's left of me to Woodlands Crematorium; tell him to see Conn Thatcher at Harker Farm in Kettleness, tell him I've gone to a better place…and tell everyone I'm sorry about all the dead folk – and the cats.'

'What is your nephew's name, spirit?' asked the vicar tentatively.

'I'm not a spirit; I'm a publican.'

'You are in spirit, my son.'

'I'm in limbo, in a grubby workshop full of dead people and motorbikes. It's hell!'

'Where you a Christian, my son?'

'I was, Father, though I must confess to serving alcohol on Sundays – quite a lot of it – and to being a werewolf.'

'You are waiting on God's judgement, my son. God forgives all sins, if you cleave to his mercy…'

'Even watering down me beer?'

Grant rolled his eyes disdainfully and shook his head.

'That is a trifle in the scheme of things,' said the vicar approvingly. 'You did what you thought was right.'

'I did it, because I could get away with it, vicar.'

'God forgives you, my son. Throw yourself upon his mercy.'

'Well, it was Budweiser, so they've probably never

noticed. I don't want to throw myself on anything in here: the whole place is filthy and covered in grease.'

'God bless you, my son, and may God forgive you your sins.'

'*No more sniffing lampposts, Lord!*' pleaded Boldwood, addressing the Almighty, and he left his earthbound representative with barely a thank you.

Their conversation was abruptly severed, saving the vicar from any further insult, when Elsie suddenly flopped forwards, just managing to put her hands out in front of her before she cracked her chin on their table. Then she vomited half a cereal bowl full of ectoplasm over the tablecloth. '*Don't break hands! I'm all right!*' she gasped, clearing her throat. When she had regained herself, she tipped back her head and took a deep breath, attempting to reconnect with her spirit guide. 'Roll-up!'

'Hold your end steady, lad, whilst I screw it in,'

'Roll-up! What you doing?' groaned Elsie, spitting out the last traces of something that looked like wallpaper paste as she fought against another wave of nausea.

'I'm nipping up the exhaust collars on the Kawasaki triple. Aydin's' holding the silencers up. Keep the bracket tight against the frame, lad; if that frigging rubber wombat falls out we'll have to start all over again. I'll be with you in a second, Else- just gotta get the bolt through the exhaust bracket and the wombat, then we're sorted. Three arm job, this is, you know; luckily, Aydin's fully qualified, just having the one to my two. D'you want me to send the next dead one through direct?'

'Just make sure he's not been licking his balls; I've got some horrible, wiry hair in me throat, from that landlord,' groaned Elsie, trying to spit a horribly springy, wiry hair out of her mouth.

'You'll like this one. He's the fella that's tekking the Kawasaki. You got plenty of protection there, so don't worry. I gotta go out a minute, I REALLY need a fag!'

'Don't you be sending me no devils, Roll-up!'

The glowing, misty fog that had been providing all the light at their table suddenly blinked out and the room began to grow darker, black shadows began to creep out of the carpet around the bottom edges of the heavy brocade curtains. Somebody began to moan.

'Grant, get over here and light this candle QUICK! An' uncork me crucifix... c'mon, lad! MOVE! BREAK HANDS EVERYBODY! HANDS ON THE TABLE!' shouted Elsie.

The atmosphere in the room quickly became quite close and uncomfortable, her sitters were conscious of an uncomfortable pressure in their ears and noses. To add to the accidental atmosphere of mirth, a choir of long-dead Spanish sailors joined the seance, shaking their chains and maracas theatrically.

'GEEV ME GOLD, ENGLEESH!' shouted a hostile, disembodied voice below the ceiling rose.

'Don't you be coming into my house and giving me orders, whoever you are. *Who are you?*' snapped Elsie, clutching her grammar-school rosary and a man-sized tissue.

'*ANTIGUO HOMBRE* WEEETH HAIR COLOUR OF STRAW... GEEV BACK GOLD OR MORE *FUEGO* I BRING YOUR HOUSE!'

All of Elsie's guests turned to look at Derek Beautimann, who blushed and tried to avoid locking eyeballs with his fellow sitters.

'You're in my house now, so unless you want zapping, chum, answer the bloody question. *What's your name?*' repeated Elsie, coming to Derek's rescue.

'"CHUM"… WHAT EEZ "CHUM"?'yelled the spirit.

'Dog food.'

'*QUE?*'

The verbal duel came to an abrupt halt as Elsie's newest spirit guest reappraised his opponent and took a moment to prepare a reply sufficient to conceal his confusion and his embarrassment at being stuck in the unfamiliar state of being lost for words. As a fairly frightening Spanish demon of several hundred years standing, Tapas-Molinos was used to being addressed a little more respectfully. But his present host was showing a worrying lack of fear and a distinct lack of deference. She also had a most formidable manner and more swagger than any other mortal he had ever met. He decided to play safe. He decided to play dumb.

'I HAVE COME WRONG HOUSE? WHERE IS ROLL-UP?' Tapas-Molinos shouted.

'He dropped you off with me, whilst he was putting some exhausts on your bike, chum. The sneaky little git,'

'*SI*, I WAIT FOR HEEM, MAKE KAWASAKI METAL HORSE, VERY FAST, VERY GOOD. MAKE GOOD STINK,' crowed Tapas-Molinos, imagining 750cc of screaming two-stroke mayhem in his grip.

'I'm not gonna ask you a third time, whoever you are. You've got one last chance or the holy water's coming out, *capiche*?' snapped Elsie, slamming a Walther PPK replica water pistol on the ectoplasm-stained tablecloth.

The invisible form of Tapas-Molinos slowly circled the table, making a slow pass over Elsie's deadly looking sidearm. He decided not to provoke another argument with a medium whose idea of a holy-water pistol was copy a of James Bond's favourite item of personal protection. Though he still dropped a golf-ball-sized lump of sulphur on Elsie's table-mat stack as a calling card and a warning. Elsie put out his smoking 'gift' with her water Walther and then blew away some invisible smoke from the end of her muzzle. Grant was tempted to showcase his best Dirty Harry, 'Do ya feel lucky, punk?' impression, but thought he had better not add another competing element to the general air of bafflement and incredulity afflicting Elsie's more delicate guests.

'I'm still waiting, laddie…' said Elsie, waving the muzzle of her holy-water pistol around in a slow, deliberate circle.

Mrs Dodson from the Society of Inner Light realised suddenly that her mouth had been wide open for almost all of Elsie's seance. She slammed it shut. She was also struggling to ignore a creeping wave of nausea caused by the ghastly pong of Duckham's Chainguard and the splash of ectoplasm, which was as authentically repulsive as anything that had ever offended her nose in the physical world.

'I AM CALLED TAPAS-MOLINOS, GUARDIAN OF THE TREASURE OF THE MAR DEL NORTE. YOU MUST RETURN GOLD – OR DIE.'

'You talking to me?' asked Elsie, doing her best Travis Bickle impression.

'NO EEZ BALD, BLOND *HOMBRE* SAT NEXT TO FAT LADY…'

'DON'T YOU BE TALKING TO ME LIKE SOME UPPITY WAITER ON THE COSTA DEL BOY, SONNY! YOU NASTY, OILY, LITTLE TWONK!'

'"TWONK"… WHAT IS "TWONK"? IS FOOD FOR

CAT?' snapped the demon, intensely irritated by Elsie's brutal verbal barbs, but even more annoyed by the thought that he was being played for a fool.

'*Tapas-Molinos* – what kind of stupid name is that? Tapas-Molinos – *my arse!* Are you taking the Michael? "Tapas-Molinos" was what I 'ad with patatas bravas an' paella in Barcelona? You're a bloody devil, aren't you? That's what you are! You can get out of my 'ouse right now, d'you 'ear me? An' you can tek yer chain-rattlin' backing singers with ya.'

Grant began to hum 'Spanish Harlem', which did not go down well with Tapas-Molinos.

There was a sudden marked increase in the smell of sulphur in the Gold Cup Lounge. It was bad enough for Tapas-Molinos that he had been temporarily offloaded into a hostile house by the man who was making him wait for his Kawasaki, but to be humiliated by a tattooed former state-registered nurse and a hairy, oversized doorman was all too much.

Tapas-Molinos exploded. 'I NO LIKE THIS PLACE; TOO MUCH SALT AND CRYSTAL. YOU ARE BAD, BAD WOMAN…' it bellowed, '*ADIOS MUJER ESPIRITU, NO PUEDO QUEDARME*[2] – PATATAS BRAVAS COSTA TWONK!'

The demon decided he was not going to force his way back to Roll-up's astral workshop without a face-saving display of childish vandalism, so he went for the decorative mirror on the back wall of the Gold Cup Lounge, blowing out the glass seconds before exiting via the front window's curtains, which he rippled theatrically – as any other self-

2 Goodbye spirit woman, I can't stay.

respecting malignant entity who has just had his dignity pricked would do in his place. Then, he threw the patio doors open and slammed them shut again with a bang that shook the whole conservatory and all Elsie's guests.

'Bloody demons! I won't 'ave 'em in the 'ouse! *You 'ear me, Roll-up?* Any more o' them and I'll be looking for a new spirit guide, an' you can do penance with some other fool! Are you listening? And where are you going?' said Elsie, looking at Derek Beautimann as he was about to stand. 'You needn't think you're going anywhere.'

'But—'

'*Grant!* Make sure Mr Beautimann's sitting down straight,' commanded Elsie. 'Right, vicar – you're up next. Your old bishop's in the wings.'

Chapter Eighteen

The Flashing Blade

A few miles south, in the lounge bar of the Shirestones Hotel – which was currently being 'run' by the former landlord's nephew, a member of the Vikings MCC from Bridlington was about to make conversation with a striking goth girl dressed as Boudicca, who was deep into a copy of Oscar Wilde's *The Picture of Dorian Gray*. Fenella Parrish, Michael's girlfriend, was unwinding after another perilous evening of battle practice with the East Yorkshire Ancient Warrior Society on Cloughton green. Her sword, Skull Splitter, was resting beside her, balanced between two stools.

'Buy you a drink, love?' asked the leather-clad man leaning against the bar rail.

'Schnapps, ta,' replied the girl without looking up.

'Got any schnapps, Ben?' asked the man, keeping his gaze on the girl and her book.

'I think so – yeah, somewhere. Give us a second, mate.'

'Any ice in that, pet?' asked the stranger, a little too assertively.

'Certainly not; it'll spoil the taste,' replied Fenella, stubbornly refusing to move her eyes from her book.

'What's your name, love?'

'Fenella is my name. Though most people call me "*that bitch with the gift shop*".'

'You've got your own gift shop?'

'It's more of a trap really, for the unwary,' She replied wearily.

'My name's Baz.'

'Hi Baz. Thank you for the drink. Very thoughtful.'

'You on your own then?'

'I'm waiting for my boyfriend actually.'

'Like you is he?'

'No, he prefers an axe.'

'And what would he say if he knew I was buying you a drink, pet?' asked Barry, trying to suppress his irritation because Fenella was still refusing to look up at him.

'Well, when he gets here after he's finished his burglary, he'll probably say that buying me a drink might have been the only thing that stopped me running you through with my war sword for being such an arrogant, self-entitled twat. This thing I nearly blunted tonight in our shield wall,' she said, drawing four feet of sharp-edged steel out of her scabbard with a dangerous flourish, 'It's about as long as your inside leg, sweetie. You can keep the schnapps for your mum.'

Barry took a step towards Fenella's table with a slightly menacing expression, but suddenly stopped when she slammed he sword blade onto her table. Then, Fenella's personal warrior rearguard Desira stomped back into the bar from the toilets, carrying a pole axe and her willow-board shield. Desira was Whitborough's own Hattie Jacques, was as broad and as tall as the Shirestones Hotel's front door with a mouth like town crier.

Baz straightened up quickly, took one look at Desira and retreated swiftly to safety in the car park.

'Is he bothering you?' asked Desira, watching Barry as he scuttled away in haste.

'Not any more…'.

'Have you got a lift home, Fen?'

'Michael and Dean are picking me up here later,' she said tiredly.

'I'll hang about until they turn up then. Just in case your pet arsehole comes back.'

'I can look after myself you know, Desira.'

'Oh, I know. I was just making sure you didn't run him through without a good excuse,' she said, waving at Baz who had glanced back briefly into their room through one of the small glass panes in door to the corridor.

'Creepy-looking bastard, that one. They're the Vikings, aren't they? The ones who were in that big ruckus at the Saltersgate Inn. I wonder if they're on bail?'

'No idea, Desira. They seem to be staying out the back, and he's the only one who's come in here. How's that knuckle of yours, sweetie?'

'It's only a scratch; it'll be reet. There's a glass of schnapps on the bar; is that for you?'

'Yes. Creepy biker bought it for me,' said Fenella with a sigh, 'before he left in a huff.' She said, patting Skull Splitter, her favourite war sword.

'Don't mind if I neck it then? Bit of a waste otherwise…'

'You're welcome to it, sweetie. Will you get me a gin and tonic, Desira? I could do with a reset after all the pushing and shoving we've done on the green tonight. Let's have a drink or two before the boys get here…'

★

A few miles north of Cloughton, Dean climbed up Charlwood estate's boundary wall with the agility of a chimpanzee, throwing his right leg over the last course of blocks and pulling himself upright until he was astride its dome-shaped coping stones. Then, he unzipped the lower compartment in his rucksack and took out a long length of nylon twine, feeding the end down to Michael, who tied it off on their watering can's handle. Dean pulled up the beer and then lowered it down the other side, whilst looking about for any patrolling zookeepers. Once Michael had dragged himself up to join Dean, they surveyed the park and re-examined their map. After parting the branches of the tree screening them from sight on the park side, they began to shin down the trunk until they were looking straight ahead at Edith the rhino's sleeping quarters. They waited silently again for several minutes in the darkness, whilst they double-checked their position and looked for any signs of human activity, before setting off with their watering can of Owd Bob. The lighting at Charlwood Zoo was kept to a bare minimum at night to enable the animals to maintain their natural sleep cycles, aiding Dean and Michael's concealment. Within a short space of time, they had reached the long side of Edith's enclosure unseen and stood listening in the shadows.

'Dean, I think she's asleep already – listen...' said Michael, whispering quietly to his colleague as they detected the unmistakeable snore of a dreaming rhino.

'That's a result! Do you want to give it a try without the beer? It's too late for plan A, innit? We can take the beer back with us.'

'Are you sure you want to take that watering can all the way back to the car?'

'Too right! I ain't pouring this away. It's Owd Bob! I'll neck it later. Are you gonna go for it then? We can't stay here too long in case we get spotted. Oh, by the way, you're carrying the beer; I'll carry the gold.'

'You're gonna finish four pints of Owd Bob after swigging the toxic potion in that flask?'

'Yeah. Why not?'

'It's a good job you're not following Richard Burton up a rock wall to sneak into the Schloss Adler,' said Michael sarcastically, referring to the nail-biting climbing scene in *Where Eagles Dare*.

'Clint Eastwood's got nothin' on me,' said Dean, grinning from ear to ear.

'How often do the patrols come past?'

'Brian said they're every hour and it's a fifteen minute circuit. It's just gone quarter past, so we've got a good forty minutes until the next sweep.'

'Okay. You stay here as lookout; I'll go in on my own.'

'Are you sure?'

'I'll be fine. I haven't got calvados and sherry on my breath. Wait here.'

Fortunately for the two punk commandos of Clash City Records, their rhino host had been prescribed a mild sedative for her dental examination earlier that afternoon and was full of the joys of sleep. With a belly full of cabbages, lettuce, spinach and fruit, she was in the best condition for tiptoeing around that they could have wished for. The rhino burglars were in luck.

Michael stood up slowly and took a step forwards, feeling the ground with his boot before he put his full weight on the grass – in case there were any brittle twigs or objects that might make a noise if they were stepped on. After a cautionary peep around the corner, he turned and shuffled forwards, flattening himself against the back wall as he moved sideways like a crab towards the service door. Soon, he was standing next to the door handle and the bolt beneath, and, crouching down, he took out a bar of soap, pushed the long pin of the bolt up hard with his fingers and began to grate it vigorously across the bolt's collars, filling in all the tiny, squeaky crevices. After a few minutes of rubbing, he was able to draw out the bolt without it making a sound. Then he opened the door a few inches and peered in.

Michael was pleased to find that, inside Edith's sleeping quarters, it was brighter than most of the nightclubs, dark cellars and haunted houses he had been creeping around in for most of his teenage years, thanks to the large, translucent, corrugated panels that covered a quarter of the cabin's roof area.

He was still going to have to tread very carefully indeed, though he was fairly confident he would be able to reach the toolbox without making a noise. There was a risk that something inside the toolbox was going to make a noise when he moved it. But there was nothing else for it, he was going to have to take the risk; it was the only variable he could do nothing about. He had his black clothes, ski mask and gloves; he had rolled on the grass outside Edith's cabin at Dean's suggestion to get rid of his own scent; and he had a scarf that had been rubbed on some of the rhino's dried dung. It was less unpleasant that he had imagined and more than worthwhile from the perspective of someone at risk of being crushed or impaled on her horn, if she should wake up. An experience he had no wish to see come true.

Luckily, he was able to find the toolbox and retrace his steps to the door without making a sound. He could hardly believe his good luck, though the first thing he did after replacing the bolt was to take his scarf off. Dean had never been so pleased to see him.

Ecstatic as they were, Dean and Michael still had one last hazard to negotiate on their way back to Amie's Mini. The forest larder of Lindsay Boldwood. Unbeknownst to them, it's packer was no longer a threat to anyone living, but the thought of meeting such a formidable and careless serial killer with a strange penchant for dog's toys was still on their minds. Even a toolbox full of gold had not erased the memory of the old lime kiln filled with body parts. Fortunately, they saw and heard nothing that might have made them break into a run on their way back to their car. It looked as though they were going to come out on top after all.

Once they were safely back in their Mini with the gold behind the back seat and a watering can full of untouched beer, the rhino commandos decided to celebrate and guzzle down a few mouthfuls before driving back to Whitborough via the Shirestones Hotel. Dean turned the ignition key, and the engine came back to life. Then something very large and hairy leapt over the bonnet and ran off down the track to the sawmill.

Chapter Nineteen

The Dog-Man Legend of Old Albert Gall

Albert took the Whitborough bus from Whitby Bus Station to the Woolpack Inn, which was equidistant from Cloughton and Charlwood Zoo, for a quiet evening's drinking; once he'd had a meal and a long, relaxing afternoon in the Endeavour bar, away from the erratic attentions of his eccentric younger sister and her hissing cat. He had made up his mind to move out the next day into a small flat at the Saltersgate Inn, until his bungalow was ready. Cecelia was far too moody and dogmatic for Albert's liking and kept threatening to call the police every time he farted. Almost as soon as he had finished using her cutlery or china it was snatched away, washed, dried and filed noisily in her cupboards with the kind of indecent haste that made him feel distinctly unwelcome. Every time he moved, her cat shrank back into its corner basket and bared its teeth at him. He had only been sharing her house for two days since being discharged from hospital and he was already at the end of his tether. Cecelia's cat felt very much the same about the old werewolf that was sharing his mother's settee.

The Woolpack Inn was a very basic, traditional moors' pub with a wide pavement of mixed flagstones and cobbles at its front, butting the kerb of the main road to Cloughton. Built in rough, milled block stone, it had a classic farmhouse pattern door: a solid ledged and braced affair with two small, stout sash windows either side; behind the door was a short corridor that opened into an open-plan bar and a restaurant, which occupied the space once reserved for livestock. Open fires in great braziers at either end of the lounge bar ensured all the pub's canine visitors a blissfully warm back and offered the customers a visual focal point for their thoughts on cold winter evenings. The furniture was spartan but comfortable, and the pub radiated the kind of ambience that only decades of lovingly applied wear and tear could buy.

Regrettably, the old pub's many charms had made little impact on Albert's nagging sense of unease and neither had several pints of Theakston's. He couldn't comprehend why he had been off his food since leaving hospital, but, oddly, he wasn't in the least bit hungry, and to add to his confusion he'd felt a strange new urge to sniff every lamp post and gate on the street. This was a temptation he'd so far managed to resist. Finally, Albert's bladder forced him to refocus his thoughts towards visiting the men's. Once inside the toilet, he walked past the white, enamelled 'weeing wall' and gutter, to save his best shoes from being spotted, and walked into the single water closet at the end, leaving the door slightly ajar. A piece of hairy string with a metal hook on the end held a wad of torn squares of news print below a crocheted sign in a glass picture frame which read, 'FER YORR COVENTENIENCE, PLES YOOSE THE NOOSPAPPER', in aggressively austere capitals. It had been carefully embroidered by a lady with dyslexia, some forty years before, and every bug and insect that could find its way between the linen and the glass had left its corpse for posterity. A dusty, stuffed ferret with one eye looked down on his cap from the cistern as he started his flow and then something very strange happened. It felt to him like something had caught fire inside the centre of his head. The unbearable heat spread quickly across his face, neck and shoulders, and raced towards his feet. Suddenly, he couldn't pull his clothes off fast enough and he fled the closet, making a dash for the cold tap at the sink with his trousers still wrapped around his ankles. Thick, matted, grey hair started to spread across his skin like a speeded up time-lapse film of ivy smothering a wall. His jaw was now throbbing so badly that he wanted to scream, but he only manage a feeble gurgle. Then, his vision started to flicker, and he fell backwards into the urinal's gutter where the electric bucks and jolts from his lycanthropic fitting fired the bleach blocks and cigarette tabs across the gents like shotgun pellets.

Within a couple of minutes, Albert's metamorphosis from homeless pensioner to urine-speckled wolf-man was complete. Steadying himself on his two new legs, he growled experimentally at the ferret on the toilet cistern to test his voice, then decided to vacate the pub to explore the back yard and lawns before the noise of his exertions attracted any human company. Because of Albert's advanced years, his body was only capable of achieving a fifty/fifty mix of man and werewolf. So, his human side was very much aware of his predicament, he was still bipedal, he had a brand-new face that might best be described as Francis Bacon's interpretation of the Hound of the Baskervilles, the eyes of a conger eel, and the kind of teeth that had absolutely no chance of coping with his favourite dry-roasted peanuts and egg fried rice. It took him a couple of unsteady attempts to negotiate the floor tiles to the back door of the pub, then he was cloaked safely in the darkness of the yard, taking in the scents drifting on the night air. There was also something pungent coming from a large, green army truck that had been parked under cover amongst some trees outside the reach of the car park's lights, but he thought no more of it. For no particular reason, he decided to head south from the Woolpack Inn towards Cloughton village and set off gingerly at first, enjoying the springy power and the long stride of his new legs until he was sprinting through the undergrowth with a new glee and purpose that he could never have imagined in his wildest dreams. It wasn't too long before he crossed the track from Cloughton sawmill, scarcely registering the dark outline of a small car beneath one of his gazelle like leaps.

★

'*What the friggin' 'ell was that thing?*' said Dean as Albert vaulted over the bonnet of the rhino burglars' black Mini, and disappeared into the trees.

'What thing?' asked Michael, peering into the small, dark gap between their seats.

'That thing that just leapt over our bonnet; didn't you see it?'

'Nope, I didn't see anything, mate. I was trying to find my seatbelt anchor. Can we just get the hell away from here ASAP [as soon as possible]?'

'It looked like a giant wolfhound!'

'So you saw a stray dog – *big deal!* There's a *psycho, cannibal serial killer* out there, and I don't wanna be here when he comes back, so shall we get going? You can phone the RSPCA about your stray wolfhound tomorrow morning.'

'I don't think they'd believe me, Mike.'

'Why not?'

'Cos the bloody thing was running on two legs,' said Dean, starting up the Mini.

'Is your door locked?'

'Yes!'

'Floor it!'

'We've still got to pick Fenella up from the Shirestones Hotel, Dean!' cried Michael as he braced his arms against the dashboard, silently praying that the Mini's strained suspension wouldn't break from another round of abuse. 'The sooner we get this gold back the better I'll feel.'

'Has she been at her thing?' asked Dean, straining to see the end of the forester's track.

'Yeah, they were practising defensive walls and circles in the meadow at the back of the chapel tonight. They've got three enactments at Whitborough Castle this summer. She's pretty good with that sword, y'know.'

'Well, I'm glad she's got it with her tonight. Here's the smooth stuff!' crowed Dean, as their headlights picked out the main road. An olive-green Bedford truck of the type the army used to transport ammunition roared past, and then the road was clear.

'We should be safe once we get back to Cloughton.'

'I bloody hope so, mate,' agreed Dean. 'The things I do for them Drake brothers. I need a bloody drink…'

'Me too. Just not that bloody poison in your flask…'

Chapter Twenty

Bert's Progress

Ever since his adoption by Burniston's anarchist commune BADCOW, Maureen Moment's rapscallion terrier, Bert, had been spoiled rotten. He had established a high position in his new pack of humans, he could share the boys' beds and sofas (sometimes he could share the girls' beds too, after his weekly bath and blow dry),and there wasn't a can of air freshener or a dish of potpourri anywhere in the former Scout huts they called home. Nor could he detect the slightest whiff of Dettol or the mango Shake 'n' Vac of which his last mama, Maureen, was so fond. There wasn't much in the way of real meat either, at least when the female humans were cooking. But he was still getting regular handfuls of corned beef, veggie sausage, and the odd steak-and-kidney pie from the boys.

His new best friend – Stigg, the jester of BADCOW – took him on long walks around the countryside, and on Sunday Gary, Penny, Digger, Cassandra, Badger, Cheesy, Mike and Stigg took him for lunch at the Hayburn Wyke, where he had his first Yorkshire pudding filled with gravy. He was a dog reborn.

The only members of the commune he didn't warm to was their führer Mary 'Shipsulk' Shipley Brown and Jim, her Albert

Speer.[3] Neither of them had ever so much as tickled Bert's ears. The first time Mary had gone home to see her parents, he had pushed her door open and dragged his bum across her pillows.

The large plot of land now occupied by BADCOW had been left to Stigg by his grandparents, and had only recently been vacated by the Sea Cadets. It was very neat, well laid out and well equipped. There was an allotment to sniff around in, a huge grass field with large sycamore trees to rest under, and as much interaction in the way of exciting ball games as his little heart could stand. The boys loved playing football with him, and he loved dashing through their ankles and leaping for whatever ball happened to be in the air. There were branches galore under the trees to grind up and he was never short of a warm lap. Best of all, there was an inexhaustible supply of smelly socks and sweaty t-shirts to curl up with. He had never slept as soundly since he was born.

The only thing that disturbed his sleep were the nightmares he'd had about his mother returning to claim him. And Mr Reynard at Bellend Veterinary Practice in Aveyou Nympton. He still had the odd flashback in which he replayed the memory of Mr Reynard's advancing towards his rear end. Bert had bitten off poor Mr Reynard's bum-inspection digit before it had the chance to do its worst. But he had finally found his Shangri-La, and nothing and no one was going to come take it away whilst he still had teeth in his head.

★

That same evening, just before Bert was due to go out for his bedtime wee, he began to growl.

---

3   A close ally of Hitler.

'What's up, fella, is there a fox outside?' asked Stigg as Bert stood bolt upright between his knees.

'What is it, Bert?' 'Why are you shaking, kid?' said Badger.

'Is he shaking?' asked Stigg, suddenly coming to attention.'

'He just shivered; I'm sure he did.'

Bert ducked underneath the sofa, and began to growl and whine.

'Must be summat outside that's got his back up – get a couple of torches,' said Stigg to Badger.

A short time later, the two punks opened the shed door and looked out over the ground separating the two huts, switching on their torches they scanned the gravel square at the end of the drive. There was a distinct lack of chirpiness from the wildlife in the surrounding trees. An unearthly quiet had descended over their field.

'That's a bit weird. The livestock's not normally this quiet unless Mary's washing her Escort,' said Badger, referring to Winnie and Nelson their goats and the commune's clucking hens.

Suddenly, they heard a deep, other-worldly growl from behind the water tank.

'There's another dog out there, Stigg! Stigg… are you all right, mate? You've gone white as a sheet.'

'That's not a dog! Watch Bert don't go out; I've got to go get summat… I'll be back in a minute.'

'All right, buddy.'

Chapter Twenty-One

Lord William Henry Warner-Woollens and the Bureau of Soot

In the days after the mysterious release of his Canadian timber wolves, Lord William Henry Warner-Woollens and his Kenyan zoo manager – Ibrahim Kinte – held a series of interviews with his staff to investigate the cause of their escape. When everyone who had been on shift that morning and the night before had been questioned properly, the only thing they knew for certain was that his wolves had still been in their enclosure on the Wednesday morning when Deborah and Simon had started their rounds at 6.30am.

The two keepers had parked their electric cart outside the wolf pen and removed the padlock on the gate's long bolt, in accordance with set protocols. The bolt itself could only be slid back if the long pin on the attached chain was pulled out of the round aperture that lined up with the other holes on the cage frame. All the cage doors to Charlwood Zoo's enclosures had the same locking mechanism and were only padlocked at night. Opening any of these, even without the padlocks, was theoretically impossible for anything with paws. Only a pair of human hands, reaching through the steel-rod trellis, could have opened the gate from inside.

Fortunately, Simon and Deborah had also recorded in the

zoo's staff communication log the disappearance from their buggy of a spare uniform and a pair of wellington boots at the end of the shift that morning. They had assumed one of the other team members had borrowed it in passing. Every person on each new shift was expected to set out with a minimum of one change of clothes.

Lord William Henry and his manager concluded that the bearded stranger he had observed through his binoculars making his way to the front of the park, dressed in a keeper's uniform, was also the person responsible for deliberately or accidentally releasing their wolves.

Luckily for the zoo, all but one of its wolves had made straight for the catering block, where the extractor fans were whirring out the scent of ten roast chickens and they were locked in the adjacent bin store by one of the catering assistants. The rebel of the pack had been shot by a tranquiliser dart just as it had finished off one of the peacocks. Unfortunately, the sterling efforts of the staff had not been enough to prevent a series of visits from the relevant regulatory authorities.

Lord Warner-Woollens received an inspector from the Department of Agriculture and Rural Affairs, his insurers and an investigative unit from the Zoo and Wildlife Park Association, all of whom brought their own questionnaires, incident forms and improvement notices.

If he had temporarily forgotten about the small gold coin locked in his desk in his private study at Charlwood Hall, the demonic guardian of the coin had certainly not forgotten about him. Unable to make anything of its last attempt at a fire in Brian Drake's damp garden shed, Quetzlcarbon Yum Taxx was determined to make the best of a good oak desk and get a proper demon-sized blaze started. As long as the lord of the manor and his butler stayed away from Charlwood's library, there was a good chance that Yum Taxx might be able to burn a lot more than the desk.

The single remaining gold coin on the Charlwood Estate began to warm, growing hotter and hotter until the Tupperware container in which it had been placed began to soften and warp – then it began to melt. The tissue around it flared up suddenly and began to eat away at the cardboard box containing his lordship's charcoal pencils. Small flames inside the oak drawer now began to draw in more oxygen through the keyhole in the lock plate, heating up the charcoal and filling the drawer with thick, black smoke. As the smoke and soot increased in density, it began to smother the flames and the fire began to falter and die, unable to draw enough oxygen through the lock-plate aperture to overcome the build-up of black smoke and soot.

Quetzlcarbon Yum Taxx was furious. Thwarted for a second time, he released a cloud of rancid chilli oil over Lord Warner-Woollens desk and began to scatter the contents of his in tray about the carpets.

Leaving a featureless blob of blackened gold stuck to the remains of a melted Tupperware dish behind, Yum Taxx left Charlwood house in a huff, through the library chimney, and went straight for the next part of the cache in the back of Amie van der Kop's Mini 1275GT, which was a few miles south in Cloughton village. Within a matter of minutes, thanks to more favourable conditions, the floor carpet in the borrowed Mini was warmly ablaze and eating into the foam of the rear passenger seat. Dean and Michael had neglected to wind their windows all the way up into the top of the door frames, leaving enough of a gap for the fire to draw in as much air as it required to set the car ablaze.

Whilst Michael and Dean, Fenella and Desira relaxed in the Shirestones Hotel's front bar, and began to unwind after their successful mission, their transport home and their precious cargo was about to explode in a ball of flame. The petrol-tank filler pipe at the back of the Mini had just reached critical temperature.

Chapter Twenty-Two

The Punk Rock Werewolf Hunters

Stigg returned to the front door of the boys' hut, with a baseball bat and a cigarette lighter. It was quite unlike any other baseball bat Badger had ever seen, because the business end was wrapped up in a great maw of rope dipped in pitch.

'Bloody 'ell, Stigg; what's that for!'

'That's for you, 'he said, 'this is for me,' he added, pulling a nine-millimetre German Luger out of his pocket. 'Let's go get the bastard.'

'Go get what? Are you out of your mind, Barnesy?'

'Nope.'

'Where d'you get that gun?' asked Badger, pointing at the pistol.

'Grandad. It came with the allotment. And a note from Grandad about werewolves…'

'Werewolves – are you mental?'

Another low, guttural growl by the water tank interrupted the boys' conversation. Then a blood-curdling howl cut out all thoughts of calling the zoo or the RSPCA. The two punks looked at each other and then looked over to Bert, who was trotting backwards and forwards between the sofa and the door, mewling and growling, stopping occasionally to lie flat on his belly and put his paws over his ears. Then he stood up and peed on the rug.

'Stay there, Bert,' said Stigg.

'Stigg… maybe we should ring the police, mate. Seriously.'

'A punk commune ringing the cops?'

'Okay, okay…Give us a torch… and light me baseball bat, would you, mate?'

'Sure I will.'

'Stigg…'

'Don't…'

★

On the opposite side of the former Sea Cadets' parade ground, Penny had just finished crimping and back-combing her hair in her room at the BADCOW girls' barrack hut and was in need of some fresh air before she started on her make-up. She took off her Sony Walkman's headphones, pressed the stop button and swapped her punk compilation tape over into her biggest ghetto blaster. Then, she drew back her flimsy calico curtains, opened her window and stuck her face out into the gloom, leaning out on her elbows as she surveyed their vegetable garden and the henhouse beyond, whilst she freshened her lungs. Her eyes settled on an odd hummock in the middle of the cabbages that she was absolutely sure hadn't been there a few hours earlier. Her first thought was that somebody had taken it upon themselves to build a new compost heap in the middle of their vegetables, but the more she thought about it, the more ridiculous it seemed. The more she squinted and stared, the more unnatural it looked. It didn't help that the light was failing, and the whole vegetable patch was in shadow. Then, suddenly, the heap growled and began to creep forwards in a very un-compost-like fashion towards the livestock pen. As quickly as she could, she grabbed her ghetto blaster, placed it on the window sill, pressed play on the cassette player and turned the big volume-control dial up as far as it would go.

*

Albert always liked to buy himself a portion of egg fried rice after a night in the pub. If it was pension day, he treated himself to king prawn fried rice. He had never contemplated eating anything feathered.

Now, here he was - on a pub night – crouching between two rows of cabbages, contemplating two live goats and a henhouse of chickens as supper. Because of his age, his human consciousness had survived his transformation from retired man of leisure to werewolf, and – as much as he enjoyed being a cantankerous, old miser – he was really enjoying his unexpected new incarnation; that was until the first few ferocious guitar chords of 'Complete Control' by the Clash erupted from a window sill on the darkened side of the hut behind him, and he had an involuntary bladder evacuation.

Sprinting away from the barrage of noise, through the canes, empty buckets and gardeners' paraphernalia, which took more than one clump of fur from his hide, he had barely got over his sudden fright when he heard a gunshot, and a nine-millimetre silver bullet hit him hard in the rump.

Chapter Twenty-Three

Car Trouble

In the small front lounge at the Shirestones Hotel, the newest members of the 'Fellowship of Gold' were about to receive some bad news from one of the more socially responsible members of the Vikings MCC.

'Anyone of youze own a dirty, black Mini wi' no front bumper?' asked the biker.

'It's ours,' replied Michael. 'Do you want us to move it?'

'It's not in our way, son. Our bikes are nowhere near it. But you might wanna tek a look at it, as soon as ya can.'

'Oh, okay. Thanks. Is there a problem?' asked Michael politely.

'You could say that, pal – it's on fire.'

*

Amie van der Kop's beloved Mini blew up just as Dean and Michael reached the back door to the Shirestones Hotel's rear sun terrace, which was between the hotel and the car park. The explosion scattered glass fragments over the gravel, as the tyres popped and collapsed like melting liquorice, feeding a rising pall of thick, black smoke. A spinning vortex of orange flame roared around the inside of the buckling car like a cyclone, eating every last combustible scrap of fabric and foam.

The four twenty-somethings stood watching silently as their transport disintegrated in a roar of flame. Some of the bikers had come out to admire the bonfire and toasted the demise of the car on its journey to Valhalla.

'*Six litres of Owd Bob*… down the pissing drain, 'slurred Dean, taking another swig of calvados and sherry from his flask. 'Friggin' liberty…'

'Petrol tank's gone, 'commented Desira drily. 'It's a waste of time putting that out. I hope you boys didn't lose anything valuable?'

'Holy crap – we're stuffed,' said Michael.

'This is *baaaad*, man!' said Dean, beginning to sway, 'I'm gotta… gonna foam, er, phone Brian.'

'Not in your state, you're not, mate, 'snapped Michael.

'Does this mean we're not going to get our hearse, sweetie?' asked Fenella, resting her chin on Michael's shoulder as they glumly watched the last glass windows explode.

An aerosol of something flammable flew up into the sky like a fire arrow, provoking an outbreak of whistles and cheers from the Vikings.

'Bastards; I'm gonna fix their bikes, 'slurred Dean.

'Oh no, you won't – we're in enough trouble already,' muttered Michael. 'Stay there; I'll go and call Brian.'

★

Brian and David Drake had just finished a gut-busting meal of Chinese food at their home on Bader Drive on the Neatsfield Estate outside Whitborough when their house phone rang. They had just opened their third bottle of pils.

'D'you want me to get that, Brian? Just in case it's any of your steroid jockeys.'

'They've stopped calling,' said Brian miserably.

'Well, they're either arranging to bump you off or they've found a new chemist.'

'Thanks for trying to cheer me up.'

'Twenny-seven Bader Drive,' said Dave into the receiver before cupping it with his hands so his next words could not be heard by the caller. 'D' you think all those bouncers found out you gave half of 'em vials of vanilla baking essence instead of bodybuilding steroids?'

'Hope not,' said Brian, whose expression of irritation turned suddenly into panic when his brother's mouth fell open.

'YOU WHAT?'

'Dave… what's the matter?'

'Where are you?'

'What's the matter? Who is it?'

'Shuuush! It's Michael. They're at the Shirestones Hotel.'

'*What's he doing there?* Dave, gimme the phone.'

'The gold was in the Mini?'

'Dave, gimme the phone!'

'It's burned out!'

'DAVE…GIMME THE PHONE!'

'Here, have the bloody phone! I'm off to Cloughton to pick up Dean and Michael.'

'Hang on! What about the police? Are the police gonna be there?'

'Dean and Michael are leaving the pub. They've asked me to pick 'em up by the chapel at the other end of the high street, as soon as I can get there.'

'Hang on – I'll come with you.'

'You'll have to stay here. Fenella and her mate are there with 'em. There's not gonna be room, Brian. I gotta take all four of 'em back. You better ring Amie and tell 'er about the Mini. She needs to cook up a story in case the cops ring 'er tomorrow – if they can still read the VIN [vehicle identification number] plate after the fire.'

'But the registration plates…'

'The plates have melted. Where's the rest of the gold now? You moved it out of the shed didn't you?'

'It's in the basement at the shop.'

'As soon as you've dropped them off, we're taking it back,' said Brian, with a face like thunder. 'I'm sick of it.'

'Back? Back where?'

'Back to the place we nicked it from. It's been nowt but a bloody curse since we found it. We're putting it back in the bloody ground tonight; I'll get us some old clothes together and summat to dig with.'

'Are you sure, Brian? You've changed your tune. We'll have to wait a while until the car cools down.'

'Damn right I'm sure. We're getting rid.'

'Does this mean you're giving up the steroid sales and service counter an' all?'

Chapter Twenty-Four

A Shot in the Dark

Stigg's second bullet took a painful chunk off the top of one of Albert's silky ears, which caused him even more agony than the stabbing ache of the silver slug lodged in his hind quarters. All thoughts of goats and chickens left his mind as he fled through the BADCOW allotment's cold frames, tubs and dustbins towards the safety of the trees at the end of their field, as Stigg and Badger skimmed their torch beams over the vegetable patch. The scent of burning car tyres and the wail of police sirens from the other end of the high street did nothing to improve their sense of dread.

'Did you get it, Stigg, that thing in the cabbages?' asked Penny from the front veranda of the girls' hut.

'I think so. Who called the police?' asked Stigg.

'I dunno. I think they're following the fire engine to the fire in the village.'

'What was that thing?'

'I dunno, Pen.'

'You'd better put the gun away, boys, in case the cops turn up. Don't worry; if that thing comes back, I've got "White Riot" ready to go on the Clash compilation tape. If anyone from the police asks about the gunshot, I'll say it's from one of my tapes. The Spaghetti Western soundtrack I got for Chrimbo.'

Michael and Dean sat glumly on a flat gravestone in the small cemetery surrounding Cloughton Chapel, as they awaited the arrival of the Drake brothers' black Saab 900 Turbo. Fenella and Desira, sensing the boys' dismal mood, took themselves off behind the chapel for a cigarette and a chat.

'Your Mike looks a bit sour,' declared Desira.

'I get the feeling they've lost something valuable in the back of the Mini, but he won't tell me what.'

'It's not their Mini though, is it?'

'No, it's Amie's.'

'Amie?'

'She's the new girl at Clash City Records. The South African police-dog handler as was – until her Doberman attacked their marching band and sank its teeth into her chief of police.'

'Sounds like my kind of dog.'

'She's got an artificial leg; it's stainless steel.'

'Really?'

'It looks quite cool, actually.'

'What happened to her leg?'

'Shark attack, Michael said.'

'Bloomin''eck! She was lucky then…'

'Well, the shark wasn't; she gouged one of its eyes out with her engagement ring, dragged it up the beach and beat it to death with a beach umbrella.'

'With one leg hanging off?'

'No! It wasn't that bad a bite, he said. She got gangrene later on, and they had to amputate.'

'Poor cow.'

'She's a bitch, Desira.'

'I'd be a bitch for less.'

'I'm probably wrong. I don't know… I actually think she's got her eye on Brian.'

'Brian? Ha, ha, ha! She's got no chance.'

'Well, I'm not telling her; I hardly know her anyway.'

'He's not… y'know…'

'What?'

'Gay?'

'Gay! Brian?'

'He doesn't have a girlfriend does he?'

'The only queen Brian's ever kissed is the one on a £20 note, Desira. He's in love with money, and he won't exactly be chuffed now he's got to buy her a new car.' Fenella tilted her head suddenly and squinted. 'Can you hear something whining?'

'No.'

'Listen…'

The two Iceni warriors stubbed out their cigarettes on a stone sill and stood listening. A few graves away, they heard a pitiful whimper and a growl behind a large block sandstone sarcophagus on a stone plinth.

'Maybe it's Amie's Doberman,' said Desira sarcastically, 'come to haunt us for slating its mistress. Should we go and look?'

'It didn't sound very friendly, Desira, maybe we should just go…'

'GIRLS! COME ON! OUR LIFT'S HERE,' shouted Michael, as he rounded the path at the back of the chapel with his fellow burglar.

His shout brought Albert's terrifying shaggy head out

from behind a tomb, into the light of the sodium lamps lining the path beside the chapel. Then Albert crawled up onto the cap stone, crouched down and stared at the interlopers.

Dean ran unsteadily into Michael's shoulder, apologised to his friend and then tried to stop swaying as he tried to focus on something he'd caught sight of amongst the graves beyond.

'*What the friggin' 'ell is that ugly, bastard thing on that grave there?*' slurred Dean.

'What?' asked Michael, looking back from the two girls to his boozed-up colleague.

'That – there!' snapped Dean, 'on that big stone lid thing.'

'It's a gargoyle, Dean,' said Michael unconcerned. 'Though it's a bit on the large side for the plinth, admittedly.'

'On my left, Desira,' hissed Fenella suddenly, drawing Skull Splitter from her scabbard. 'Get to the car, boys, now!'

'*Holy shit…* it's alive!' gasped Michael, staring at the gargoyle that had come to life.

Albert growled, tilted his head and scratched his ear with his hind leg.

'Get to the gate, boys' hissed Desira, bringing up her willow-board shield to guard Fenella's left side. 'Don't run, walk.'

Dave Drake lit a cigarette to calm his nerves and looked back in his rear-view mirror down the high street at the flickering reflections of the fire engine and police car lights playing on the cottages and the Shirestones Hotel. Suddenly, all four of his passengers seemed to be trying to jump into his Saab at the same time. Michael went in like an oiled sardine, but Dean couldn't quite get his legs in the right position until Desira kicked him from behind and threw herself in on top of him.

'Are you in some sort of bleeding hurry? Whatever happened to ladies first?' groaned Dave.

All three of them ignored his comment and craned their necks to check on Fenella, who was feeling for the Saab's door pillar with her free hand whilst keeping her eyes on the thing behind the chapel gate and holding her sword out in front of her.

Fenella backed slowly into the front passenger seat, drew in her sword and slammed the heavy door behind her as fast as she could.

'It's still behind the gate in the churchyard, Fen,' said Desira, peering out of the Saab's small rear window,' I think we're safe for the moment.'

'Safe? Safe from who Jimmy Savile?' muttered Dave, turning to look at the three fugitives on his back seat. 'Are you pissed again, Dean?'

'Dave!' cried Michael.

'What?'

'Drive! Get us out of here!'

'Calm down, the cops aren't anywhere near us. I want to see when the fire engine leaves, and I'm finishing me fag,'

'David?'

'Yes, Fenella?'

'Do you see what's looking at us through the church gates?.'She said, tapping the passenger window very slowly and deliberately with a purple fingernail.

'OH MY GIDDY AUNT! Get your belts on!'

★

Albert didn't really want to eat or bite anything human. He had only chased the four young people out of the graveyard because they had disturbed him when he was feeling sorry for himself. He had just given them his best evil growl as their getaway driver started the car when another gargoyle stepped out from behind the First World War memorial obelisk and brought a Mossberg special-forces shotgun up into to his shoulder. Dudley Kingcombe had finally caught up with him and was one shot away from salvaging his reputation as the deadliest bandy-legged Devonian in Yorkshire. Albert's bowels let go for the second time in less than an hour, and then Dudley's shotgun boomed. Poor Albert no longer had any use for his bowels or anything else.

*

Fenella saw their ugly pursuer's head suddenly disintegrate in a great red cloud, and then she was clutching the door handle and bracing her feet as Dave Drake launched his Saab towards Whitborough as though he were driving a getaway car from an armed robbery.

*

Dudley Kingcombe watched the Drake brothers' car streak away, then walked forwards and looked at the aftermath of his handiwork with quiet satisfaction, deciding there was no immediate need to unsheathe his Bowie knife to remove the head of his kill, as the head had been turned into a huge, red spatter of skin scraps and gore spotted across the flagstones of the path. He kicked the corpse, more out of habit than necessity, as the final symbolic act of a job well done, but Albert was already irreversibly extinct. Dudley's soldier's instinct told him that there was no chance of the occupants of the car returning any time soon, so he lowered his gun and sat down on a convenient grave.

Dudley took off his sniper's camouflage shawl, removed his camouflage bush hat, said a quick prayer over the deceased, made an apology to the long-dead soul whose tomb he had sat on, licked some small droplets of rain off his lips and wiped his forehead with the back of his hand. He applied the safety catches on his Mossberg and his long-barrelled .357 Magnum, emptied their magazines, and pulled out a heavy-duty plastic body bag, and put on a pair of thick, black Marigold gloves.

★

Dudley got down to business in full view of Inspector Marshall and his freshly bandaged colleague, who were sitting in their car, in the shadow of the schoolhouse opposite, with their mouths agape. Then one of the policemen decided he needed the head flushing power of a Fisherman's Friend, to clear his thoughts and started to rummage in the drawer of his door.

'It looks like they got the right man for the job,' said Inspector Marshall, as he watched Dudley's post-execution ritual from the comfort of his Ford. 'Even if he does walk like he's got a football between his legs.'

'D' you think our lot heard that shotgun ?' asked Broadhead.

'I hope not, George; I want to see what he does next. He's just taken a meat cleaver and some bags out of his holdall.'

'My dad used to tell me there were no such things as monsters,' muttered Broadhead.

'He can't have been a copper then, can he?'

'To think I was scoffing at the landlord of the Shirestones Hotel before I walked into that sword pommel. It turns out I'm the bloody fool. I don't think I'll ever get a good night's sleep again after seeing that thing. Thank God we went on the sick.'

'I must admit, George, I was wavering about signing off for a while. It's just not something I ever thought I'd do. I always thought I'd be the last man standing – out of a sense of duty, y'know, more than anything. It's ingrained, isn't it? And then you get caught up in a mess like this. But after seeing this fella in action, I'm absolutely solid. We're well out of it, George. Did you ever get that other tape of the ghost in the lobby from Barry?'

'I signed it out when you were suspended. I was sat in our office, copying those records you asked for, and D'Ascoyne comes in bristling just as it was playing. He shit himself. He couldn't get out the office fast enough. I watched it at least three times. It looked genuine to me.'

'Oh it's genuine, all right. Barry checked it, copied it and had it sent to the lab in York too. Came back as clean as a whistle.'

'So then, just to summarise, since the Easter bank holiday the borough's had werewolves, armed terrorists, Satanists, at least one professional gunman over there, a fortune in gold, a sunken ship, corpses galore, a whole ward of seriously injured cyclists, a demolished house, a wrecked seafront, a massacre in Crescent Moon Kebabs, two dead Land Rovers, a pile of rubble with two dead gangsters spread around underneath it, and a gigantic brawl with medieval weapons at the Saltersgate Inn. What a bloody mess…'

'It's a good job we're on sick leave, isn't it, George? Or we'd have a bloody ulcer each, as well as the bandages.'

'Are we following that lot in the Saab?'

'There's no need. I know where that Saab's going. At least three of that lot work in that record store in Market Square. The one that kids are too scared to go in. They've got a waxwork of Rasputin holding a Luger and a bottle of Ouzo just inside the front door. It pretty realistic by all accounts…'

'Brian Drake's place!' Doesn't he fence steroids to doormen?'

'Not for much longer…He's in a bit of bother with some of his clients.'

'Right, George. Who – or what – do we follow? The bow-legged sniper over there or the Drake taxi to Bader Drive? As you're the expert on werewolves, I'll leave it up to you.'

'Let's follow that Saab.'

'Bader Drive it is then. I've got a feeling that car's gonna see a bit more action later. Our big-game hunter over yonder's got a bit of clearing up to do.'

Chapter Twenty-Five

A Delicate Conversation

'Amie… it's Brian. How are you?'

'Brian…What are you calling me for exactly?'

'Well… it's… the thing is, Amie, your…'

'It's because you've got some bad news for me, isn't it? I'm guessing it's about my Mini, is it, Brian?'

'Funny you should say that, Amie. I'm glad you're taking this so well,' said Brian carefully, being mindful that he was talking to a former South African police-dog handler who had battered a shark to death with a beach umbrella.

'Taking what well? Those twerps have crashed my car, haven't they? That's what you're calling for, isn't it? To tell me my car's a wreck.'

'Everyone's fine, Amie…'

'It's just my car that's wrecked…'

'In a manner of speaking.'

'What's happened to it, Brian?'

'I'll make sure you're all right, Amie.'

'Too bloody right you will, Brian.'

'Absolutely not! I mean, um…'

'*What?*'

'Amie… can…'

'Where is it?'

'It's a little crisp.'

'I didn't ask you what happened to it, I asked where it was. What do you mean a little crisp?'

'It caught fire in the Shirestones Hotel car park, in Cloughton.'

'Oh! That's bloody fantastic, that is, Brian!'

'I need you to report it stolen to the police. Now.'

'Why, Brian?'

'It's quite important that you report it stolen, Amie, as soon as possible.'

'Who for? You or me?'

'Both of us. And for Dean and Michael, of course.'

'You realise I used to be in the police, don't you, Brian?'

'In South Africa, Amie…'

'"In South Africa" – what's that supposed to mean?'

'Well, in South Africa, you have armoured cars and armoured troop transporters, with turrets and bloody great machine guns. We've got Ford Escorts. Our police are a little more subtle.'

'Is that why you've got killer Alsatian police dogs and lead-lined truncheons?'

'I'm trying to protect us all, Amie. We're all relying on you to cover for us. Please?'

'You can certainly rely on me to kill you when I find out why and I don't approve. Hang-up, NOW.'

'Yes, of course; I'm so grateful you've seen this from my perspective, Amie.'

'I want a thirty percent wage rise, effective immediately; four weeks' paid holiday; and the full value of the car, plus fifty percent. Don't make me wait.'

Brian didn't get the chance to haggle, because his phone suddenly went dead.

Chapter Twenty-Six

The Return of the King(combe)

Dudley Kingcombe's strong sense of duty and professional pride would not allow him to contemplate leaving Yorkshire until he had restored his standing in the eyes of the men and women of Whitby and Kettleness, who had hired him to rid them of their predator, even if it meant incurring more inconvenience and expense.

The fact that his host had got to his target first and dispatched it with nothing more sophisticated than a very sharp cutlass had really irked Dudley. It had also been quite a shock to Conrad Thatcher that fate had chosen him to kill the beast of Kettleness, but Conrad was at least mature and worldly wise enough to deal with whatever life threw at him without drama or protest. He was a proud Yorkshireman – and, being a Thatcher, he had inherited a damned good arm.

In marked contrast to his host Conrad Thatcher's heroic effort, Dudley's only contribution to the community of Kettleness on his first night as their guest had been a £2,000 bill for the damage done by one stray bullet to the home of the man he was now forced to hunt down as a werewolf. Being scooped up by a police Land Rover and breaking his thumb on its roof bracket had not helped to diminish his sense of injustice.

When Albert Gall had unconsciously revealed his new lycanthropic identity to Dudley on his bed in Whitby Hospital, Dudley had panicked and fled, temporarily unable to face the awful reality of what he had to do to redeem himself and complete the contract for which he had been employed. But it was still a better reality than the fate awaiting him at home in Devon. The thought of being made to court Honiton's most fertile and forceful divorcee, Ella Furnish, just to please his mother had given him a whole new perspective. Going home was not a reality he wished to contemplate.

Dudley decided to stay in Yorkshire, preserve his precious virginity and hunt werewolves until his mother's choice of daughter-in-law had lost interest in his reproductive glands. It was a much safer prospect that being forced to breed with a woman whose only redeeming feature was her ability to put a sheep on its back faster than a patch of black ice.

So, Dudley had followed Albert in his Bedford truck to the Woolpack Inn and waited in the trees for Albert's moonstruck alter ego to emerge. He had tracked him to the BADCOW compound in Cloughton and then to the chapel after Albert was wounded. It was time for him to choose a close-combat weapon to end the chase. It was time for Dudley to unwrap his favourite guns: a Mossberg special-forces shotgun and his showpiece long-barrelled .44 Magnum pistol. He also had some special ammunition for his Magnum just to make sure, if there was anything left of Albert once the shotgun's solid-slug, one-ounce ingots had left the barrel of his Mossberg.

Chapter Twenty-Seven

A Very Fine Dog Indeed

Once the excitement of seeing off the gigantic, mystery carnivore in their vegetable garden had worn off, the boys of BADCOW – and several of their friendlier female associates – did what every self-respecting young punk rocker does on a Friday night: they went to the nearest welcoming pub – the Three Jolly Morris Men in Burniston – to get drunk.

The more politely dressed drinkers at the bar seemed more animated than usual, mainly because they had a new topic of conversation and were determined to uncover the definitive account of the latest turn of events in their domain, in order that they could all have a really good grumble and have positive proof that the world really was coming to an end.

'They'll be a reckoning soon. Mark my words,' said Burniston's greatest bore, Peter Farley. 'A gunshot in Burniston,' he muttered, 'a bloody car bomb at the Shirestones Hotel and – *on top of everything else* – a gunshot at Chapel End 'ere…'

'And no kebabs, Peter! Now, that's the real tragedy.' said Margo the landlady, before her most irritating customer could finish his monologue.

'It weren't a car bomb – it were a Mini wi' a cracked fuel

pipe. That's what the fire-engine crew reckoned. As for them lads at Crescent Moon Kebabs, we read all about that in the papers,' explained Claire the barmaid.

'The Turkish mafia in Leeds, weren't it?' queried Colin Friend, Burniston's postman. 'Mad lot o' bastards, they are…'

'And that's what 'appens to you if you eat garlic and fried onions all your life!' asserted Peter.

'What, you disappear into thin air like a fart in a hurricane?' asked Rory.

'Language please, Rory!' admonished Margo.

'Sorry, Margo. I think we've all heard worst, especially the colourful young lads and lasses over yonder,' he said, nodding towards the BADCOW tables by the window.

★

'I just realised, I haven't seen Bert since he hid under the sofa,' said Badger to Stigg.

'Did you scrub the rug?' Stigg asked.

'No, not yet. I just hung it on the line.'

'We'll have to wash his pee out, y'know; it'll stink otherwise. He'll turn up, Badge. He's probably found a dead thing to roll in.'

★

Bert, BADCOW'S rapscallion Parson terrier was utterly content. He had a nice, dry patch of werewolf dung drying in the fur between his shoulder blades; he'd had sweet potato, broccoli and turkey-mince mash for tea; and he'd made a successful territorial sortie into the unoccupied bed chamber of his only adversary in the BADCOW girls' hut: Mary Shipley Brown, 'Anarchy Mary', the self-appointed general secretary of the commune.

Bert was surrounded by the spoils of Mary's make-up bag. Her precious Monsoon 'signs of the zodiac' quilt cover was now a stinking ruin streaked with lipstick, mascara and the body parts of a desiccated rat that Bert had found underneath the hut's floor joists. To add insult to injury, Bert had torn Mary's tampons from their packets and dropped them into her fish tank, where they had formed a small reef of fluffy, white buoys. As far as Mary was concerned, it was going to be the reef the broke the camel's backpack.

He had just rolled on his back, and was showing a full set of teeth and some other things when Mary opened her door and cried out in horror. She held her nose as she tried to take in the full horror of Bert's raid on her sanctuary. Then she tripped and knocked herself out on her bookcase.

Chapter Twenty-Eight

The Fellowship of the Gold

'Can I drop you two girls somewhere?' asked Dave, easing off the accelerator pedal.

'Yeah, the Battle of Stamford Bridge?' Slurred Dean, teasing Desira and Fenella, who were still dressed to kill in their Saxon warriors' outfits.

'Do you know what Fenella calls her sword, Dean?' asked Desira sarcastically.

'No.'

'Skull Splitter,' said Desira.

'Uh-huh.'

'I call my poleaxe "Drunk Punk Arse Crusher",' She added.

'No kidding,' said Dean, looking pale. 'Dave?'

'Yes, Dean…' began Dave.

'Stop the car, mate. I think I need to puke.'

Dave drew up in a screened lay-by outside Aveyou Nympton, got out and helped Michael extract himself from the car, so Dean could clamber out and find a spot amongst the bushes to retch.

'What's up with Beadle, Mike? He's not normally this much of a pushover. Are you going soft in your dotage, Beadle?' asked Dave, waving at Dean. He didn't get a very polite response.

'Four things,' said Michael, 'In reverse order, that gargoyle thing in the chapel graveyard, a big hip flask of calvados and sherry, some huge gulps of flat Owd Bob from a watering can, and a pile of body parts near the wall of Charlwood Zoo. That's enough to make anybody retch, including our own Keith Richards of punk rock over there.'

'He hasn't been eating body parts, has he? I know he's crackers but he can't be that mad.'

'No, Dave. It wasn't meat from the zoo. We just found the missing staff from Crescent Moon Kebabs. They were piled up in an old lime kiln and all torn up by some psycho. And there were some tennis balls.'

'Are you 'aving me on?'

'No.'

'Let's take a walk for a minute, away from the car. Tell me what happened to the Mini. Cos Brian and I have got to go back for the toolbox before dawn. We're gonna rebury that gold before it finishes us off. It's friggin' cursed.'

'I take it I'm not going to get my hearse, if you're going to be burying the very same thing that was going to pay for it?'

'I'm afraid so.'

'I trust I'm going to get some recompense for risking my life and – I might add – risking arrest for breaking into a rhino's stall at Charlwood Zoo, am I?'

'Do you fancy a Ford Capri?'

'Is it black?'

Chapter Twenty-Nine

(Ahm Gonnae Be) 5OO Miles

Barnett Crosbie and his bodyguard, James 'Jamesy' Stone, arrived at Hull's ferry-terminal car park in their stolen Ford Fiesta, just as the fire brigade in Whitborough began to dampen down the blazing heap of rubble and charred wooden beams that was all that remained of their former nightclub – Mystery City. The nightclub that the two gangsters had booby-trapped and fled. They had just completed the first stage of an elaborate plan to deceive any potential pursuers by laying a false trail to Hull's ferry port. However, their actual destination was Spain – via Liverpool, the Isle of Man and then a small port in the Republic of Ireland – from where one of Barnett's contacts was to take them by fishing boat to a small resort on Portugal's Atlantic coast. But, first, they needed to steal another change of clothes and a new vehicle for the next leg of their journey.

'We need tae find a sports centre, Jamesy, so we can get a shower an' a change o' clothes, pal,' explained Barnett.

'Someone else's?' queried Jamesy.

'Aye. Eff we can fix oorselves up. A new car wudnae go amiss. Sumthen' tae get uzz tae the Mersey the neet.'

'What'll we dae wi' thess?' asked Jamesy, tapping the dashboard of the Fiesta, 'we're nae gonnae torch this too, eh?'

'Huh! No focken' chance. No' in a focken' ferry-terminal car park. Put yer gloves on an' wipe doon everything in here; ahm no' leaven' nae prints, y'ken? Then we'll find a caff an' get some grub.'

'Nuthen' like a gudd, wee arson for belden'up an appetite, eh, Barn?'

'Are ye looken' forward tae Spain, Jamesy?'

'Too focken' right. D'ye thenk they'll let uzz have a wee club when we get oor new papers?'

'A club?' A rock club? Ahm no' having another focken' rock club – no focken' way.'

'Ah meant a little wee bar, y'ken? White wolls, one o' them vine creepers on a begg wee trellis for shade, terracotta tiles on the flooer, ootside balcony, mosaic-tiled tables… Somewhere you could take a lassie.'

'Ah didnae thenk ye were tha' focken' soft, Jamesy.'

'Ahm no'! Ah jusht want a wee place ah can eat ma paella wi' oot feelen'like a twat.'

'Ye can buy yersell' a bar like tha' wi' enuff coin, Jamesy, but I'll tell ye – whitewash an' splinters disnae fly wi' the lassies, pal. What they want is lots o' chrome, red-leather benches, black ceilings wi' spinnen' lights an' lots o' mirrors – an' begg, glass ashtrays.'

'Barn, ah dinnae want tae set in a focken' English disco in Spain. Ah want some culture. Donkeys wi' straw hats tae carry ma shoppen', fried onion an' chorizo sandwiches, a fountain tae watch, an' a row o' them fancy focken' cacti, y'ken?'

'Are ye sure ye dinnae want tae go tae Mexaco?'

'Mexaco? Mexaco? Why the fock wud ah wannae go tae Mexaco! It's no' like Spain!'

'Aye, whatever, Jamesy. When Aberdeen goes tae Spain,

they didnae want tae sit enn a focken' stable or a focken' Spaghetti Western bar.'

'Ya dinnae thenk the punters enn Spain want tae drenk like Clent Eastwood – the man wi' no name?'

'No. They dinnae want tae get caught up enn a focken gunfight, unless they cum from focken' Essex.

'*Oh* aye…'

'Ah thenk we shud get shum focken' braykfust, pal. Jusht remember, tell we get tae Spain, we're no' the men wi' no names.'

★

Demi's Caff on Hull's Ferryport Road did one type of meal – an all-you-can-eat all-day breakfast – in the no-nonsense venue of an old-school Portakabin. It's only concession to sophistication was chequered paper napkins – blue and white, or red and white – and a big, laminated poster of *The Pride of Hull*. A traction engine that looked as though it had been built by serious men who liked their engineering heavy. The words, 'could I see the menu' had only ever been spoken by a man whose guide dog had dragged him inside.

Demi came from Bonar Bridge. She had always wanted to go to Spain, but had only made it as far as Hull's ferry port because of a problem with some unspent convictions. Neither could she fly, since she had knocked out the supervisor at the KLM check-in desk in Manchester who had pressed her to book an extra seat so that both of her buttocks could fly. Demi was a woman in limbo. She was unemployable (unless it was casual) but rich in initiative. When Barnett and Jamesy arrived in Hull early that morning, it was not just love at first bite. It was almost her lucky day.

Chapter Thirty

Strong Words and Fisticuffs at Demi's Transport Caff

'Youze fust, Jamesy. Ahm gonnae case the car park. Tell the cook tae leave the tea bag enn ma mug; ah like ma tea strong, no' like focken gnat's pess, reet?' asked Barnett.

'Aye, Barn. Can ah have yer fried bread?'

'Aye, as long as ye get me another two hash broons.'

★

The four dockers in dungarees and donkey jackets, seated in the top right-hand corner of the Portakabin, barely noticed Barnett's companion Jamesy stride up to the counter and put down his Snap-on toolbox, big men with toolboxes being a common sight in Demi's Caff. They were more interested in finishing off their breakfasts and reading their newspapers. Jamesy, looking hungry and gormless, barely drew a glance.

★

'Aye, what'll it be, son?' asked the tough-but-comely-looking girl behind the apron.

'Two teas an' two specials. Oh, an another helpen' o'

fried bread an' hash broons, hen,' said Jamesy, winking at his fellow Scot and giving her a friendly smirk.'

'Are ye wenken' a' me, son?'

'Aye! Anyone who cooks a spread as gud as thess smells deserves a wenk.'

'A wenk ezzett? Are ye' from Aberdeenshire, then?' asked Demi curiously.

'Aye,' said Jamesy, hopping from one foot to the other.

'The loo's there,' said Demi, on noticing her latest customer was doing a half-jig on the floor.

'Ah no! Ahm jusht hungry!' said Jamesy laughing.

'Ah've never seen ye before,' said Demi, as she wrote out a chit for the cook.

'Oh, aye. Ett's ma fust time enn Hull. Ahm off tae Spain, by the way.'

'Spain, ezzett? Lucky sod.'

'Aye. Ah focken' love Spain. Sorry, ah didnae mean any disrespect, hen.'

'Which part o' Spain?'

'To tell ye the truth, hen, Ahm no' shure yet. Ah jusht cannae stay heer enn England, y'ken?'

'Ah know jusht what ye mean. Ahm Demi, by the way. Five hundred fantasy miles frum Bonar Bridge.'

'From the Bridge! Champion! So was ma mum. God rest 'er fists.'

'What's yer name, big man?'

'Jamesy.'

'D'ye want an extra sausage – on the house?' asked Demi, winking back at Jamesy. 'I love a gud cresp banger, me.'

For the first time in his life, James Stone blushed – and fell in love.

'Do ye want a lift, pet – tae Spain, ah mean?'Said Jamesy, not quite sure what he was doing or why he was asking.

'Are ye asken'?'

'Aye.'

'Tell me about it, stud,' said Demi, putting out her cigarette with an erotic twist. Then, in one of those rare moments when fates align, and the everything in creation seems to rush forwards to flatter and guild two lonely hearts, John Travolta's unforgettable duet with Olivia Newton John burst out of the caff's lard-spattered radio.

Then Barnett walked in the door and shook a bunch of car keys at the beaming face of his partner in crime, before thrusting them in his pocket. 'Ah've got us a wee ride, Jamesy.'

'Champion, Barn. Barn, thess ezz Demi. Demi's from the Bridge,'

'The bridge? What bridge? The bridge over the River Kwai?'

'Bonar Bridge,' replied Demi, deadpan.

'Very nice,' replied Barnett acidly. 'Dedd ye order me ma focken' braykfust, Jamesy, or have ye just been playing wi' yersell'?'

'Aye, Barn, the cook jusht got the chits,' said Jamesy grinning, 'Barn, Demi's going tae Spain too.'

'Ezz she now?'

'Aye, all the way.'Jamesy smiled.

'And what's it got tae do wi' us?' asked Barnett.

'Yer friend here offered tae tek me to Spain,' said Demi, 'but ah didnae realise he meant a threesome.' She turned away from Barnett's hostile aura to rattle the deep-fat fryer.

'No, hen! Barnett's ma boss, see; well, we're partners now, aren't we, Barn?' declared Jamesy.

'Jamesy, where's ma focken' tea? Ah've just spent ten minutes getting uzz a ride and ye hav'nae even got uzz a brew!'

'I've been getting acquainted wi' Demi, Barn!'

'Oh, aye; no tea for yer boss then,' said Barnett.

'His boss, are ye?' Demi enquired.

'Aye. What's ett tae ye?' asked Barnett contemptuously. He realised too late that he had said the wrong thing to the wrong woman – Demi being the wrong woman for most cautious members of the opposite sex.

The head of one of the men in donkey jackets swivelled around like the gun turret of a tank, stopping to listen to the developing conversation. Amongst his colleagues, cards and newspapers were put down and ears cocked.

'Ye look like an anaemic preck tae me,' said Demi, 'Run along, wee man. Ye can leave your friend here…'

'YE FOCKEN WHAT?' snarled Barnett, turning a healthy shade of red in the face.

'Ah'll tell ye something else too: they're ma focken' car keys! BOYS! SEE THIS PRECK OUTTA MA CAFF!' yelled Demi.

The four large dockers stood up, made their way to the counter, tapped Barnett on the shoulder and pointed to Demi's outstretched hand.

'I'll be having ma keys now, pal. Then ye an yer mate can sling yer hook,' growled Demi.

'Do as the lady says, gents,' said the largest docker, examining Barnett with the practised eye of a regular brawler, 'nice and slow.'

Jamesy dipped at the waist to pick up their toolbox, then a hand closed on his arm.

'You can leave that,' said one of the other men.

Barnett prodded Jamesy with his elbow – which was his usual pre-fight signal – before he tossed Demi's keys into the air, drawing the eyes and the attention of the men. As the keys soared over the display of sweets and snacks, Barnett brought his knee up into the crotch of the biggest and most dangerous of their opponents, and stabbed him under the chin with a good, stiff biro, forcing him backwards into the arms of his friend behind him.

At the same moment, Jamesy drove his upper forehead into the bridge of the nose of the man holding his arm, followed up with an open-palm strike to his jaw, and then he brought his right arm back high, bringing his elbow across onto the ear of the man to his right, bursting his eardrum and knocking him senseless, only half a breath after the man's first punch had bounced harmlessly off his shoulder. Jamesy followed up by thumping the temple of the man trying to crawl out from underneath Barnett's writhing victim, as Demi stomped around the counter's corner and rushed a swing at his boss. As good as it was, it was just another bad punch for a man who had spent his whole life getting the better of much larger and angrier assailants; Barnett simply dodged her arm by stepping neatly aside, grabbed the shoulder seam of her overalls as she fell past him and added to her own momentum by giving her a helping shove. She flew across two table tops before dipping and striking the edge of a third with her forehead. The cook, not wanting to go the way of his other customers, put up his hands and shrugged his shoulders.

'Ye can feed our braykfusts tae these twats when they wake up, son. Y'ken?' said Barnett, addressing the cook. 'We'll no' be staying for another tea, by the way,' he continued, taking his foot off the neck of the man with the biro stuck in his chin, just as he passed out.

'Barn?' Jamesy asked.

'Aye Jamesy?'

'D'ye thenk we've got time for a sandwich? I'm really focken famished.'

★

After Barnett and Jamesy had finished a hearty all-day-breakfast in one of the many other eateries on Ferryport Road and begun to relax, the conversation returned to the circumstances of their first attempt to buy their first meal 'on the road'.

'How long's ett been, Barn?' asked Jamesy, examining his right hand for cuts and nicks.

'Ah was worried we were gonnae get oll the way tae focken' Liverpool wi' oot a gud dust-up. Ett must be nearly a month sense ma last punch.'

'Hull's come through for uzz, eh, Barn?'

'Aye, jusht what we needed, Jamesy. Ye cannae get too soft enn this game.'

'D'ye thenk we'll see some more trouble, then?' asked Jamesy, brightening up.

'Once we get tae Liverpool, Jamesy, ah can focken' guarantee ett. Ah can jusht aboot feel masel' coming back tae life, pal,' added Barnett with a grin.

'Remember tha' last fella ye felled in tha' toon hall, eh?'

'Aye, well enuff. He shouldnae have colled me an entrepreneur. Focken' cheek.'

'Dedd ye find oot what it meant?'

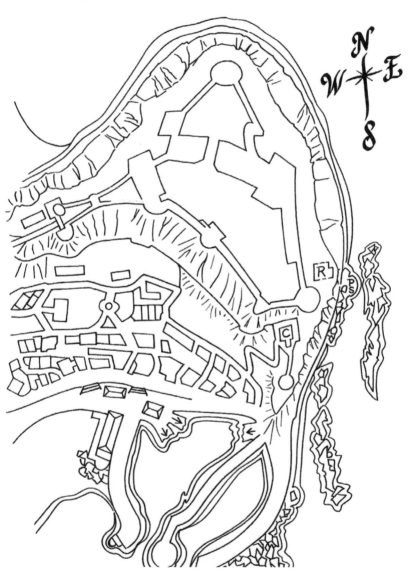

Whitborough on Sea Old Town and Harbour, 1983

Whitborough on Sea

Principal street index

The final instalment of the first series of the Whitborough novels will follow.